WILLIAM S RUSSELL

The Guardian of the Dragon

Newhouse Creative Group

First edition

ISBN: 978-1-945493-14-0

This book was professionally typeset on Reedsy.
Find out more at reedsy.com

Prologue

Steven heard the *whoosh* as the portal collapsed behind him. They had made it back alive. The Seeker, formerly an Egyptian priest named, Sonchis, and Bastet, Steven's Egyptian cat, had also survived. Who knew the cat his parents had brought home from Egypt would turn out to be an Egyptian Goddess with a mind of her own? Steven had thought he was protecting his pet, but now wondered if it was the other way around? She'd saved his life. That was for sure!

Being selected by the ancient Egyptian Gods to undertake these dangerous missions had taken Steven by surprise. He had opened one of his parent's files on Egyptian Spirits and suddenly found himself being pulled into a life and death struggle. Sonchis, and the other ancient Egyptian priests had discovered a prophecy—a prophecy that said a boy would eliminate the evil Guardians concealed around the world by the Ruler of Darkness to destroy mankind. The prophecy declared that if this boy could free the souls of the Guardians then he would be able to destroy the evil Ruler himself, the demon responsible for his parents' deaths.

Steven survived the first quest into the tomb of Seti I in the Valley of the Kings, but just barely. He shivered at the thought of getting trapped in a tomb again, battling the monsters protecting the Guardians.

Unless he could find a way to defeat the Guardians, and their powerful ruler, the world was doomed.

But was Steven ready?

Chapter 1

Steven backed toward the Portal, his eyes on the Devourer, one of the Dark Ruler's slaves, as the massive monster struggled to remove the burning torch from her throat where he had lodged it when she attacked him. The flame from the phosphorous flare was shooting out of the wound in the side of her neck. She let out a hair-raising scream.

The portal slammed shut and Steven was hurled back from Egypt to the safety of his aunt's house.

Steven could still hear the Devourer's agonizing screams in his brain as he stepped into his parents' laboratory. Rushing over to the computer tower, Steven pressed the off button. The Portal collapsed with another whoosh.

Exhausted from his near escape, Steven dropped into his dad's black leather chair. He was covered in dust and sand from spending hours searching the tomb of Seti I for the Guardian, and from his battle with the Devourer.

"Is your arm damaged, Steven?" The Seeker, the spirit of Sonchis, an ancient Egyptian priest, an ally in the battle against the Dark Ruler, asked telepathically, as he floated over to the boy.

"Oh! My arm?" Steven asked, still dazed.

"You have a long gash down the sleeve of your jacket. Did she cut you with her claws?"

Steven pulled off the denim jacket and examined it. He then checked out his arm. "I'm fine. Not a scratch on me. I was lucky," he said, seeming to come to. "I can't believe I had the courage to fight such a ferocious beast. I guess when you realize it's either 'kill or be killed', you just do what it takes."

"You did well, boy of the prophecy." The Seeker let out a rare smile.

The air in the basement was cool and comfortable, unlike the humid hot air three hundred fifty feet below the Valley of the Kings, in the tomb of Seti I, in Egypt. His breathing was returning to normal.

Bastet, his cat, interrupted her grooming. *I did well too,* she said with a meow.

Shu, the Egyptian Wind God, another member of the small team, shot several small bursts of wind in Bastet's direction to help her get rid of the sand clinging to her usually shiny black coat. But the blast blew Bastet onto the computer table. "Meow," she screamed, lashing out with a paw. *Don't mess with a goddess,* she spat at the wind God circling around her like a small tornado.

"I'll have to clean the dust off the keyboards and monitors later," Steven grumbled.

"You guys always make such a mess!"

The cat let out a loud squeal.

Steven laughed, as the cat raced around, searching for the source of the wind that was teasing her.

"Shu, this is no time to play." The Seeker placed his hand on the boy's shoulder. "I could not have freed the Guardian from the Dark Ruler's control without your help, Steven." He sighed. "I must admit, at first, I questioned the gods' selection of you for this dangerous task. Now I see their wisdom was far greater than mine. You are the boy of the prophecy."

Steven still didn't love the idea that the whole fate of mankind was resting on his ability to defeat the evil Dark Ruler. He worried about the danger to his Aunt Celia too. "Does the Ruler know who I am, or where I live?" he asked.

"No. I do not believe so. At any rate, with your help, I was able to defeat him once and for all."

"Are you sure about that?"

The Seeker smiled. "When I left him, all bundled up in threads of incense, poisonous to him, Shu, our friend, stood watch to assure he did not escape and come after you."

"Thank you, Shu," Steven said. "You are a good friend." He felt the warm touch of a gentle breeze on his face.

The Seeker nodded. "Shu confirms that the Ruler was still bound up and unable to escape from where we left him—"

"But Shu is here now," Steven interrupted.

"I assure you, you and your aunt are safe." The Seeker pulled at his long gray beard. "Remember, Steven, even if he could escape, the Dark Ruler, even with all his considerable powers, can't step out on the earth's surface. That is why he must send his slaves to capture you. But of course, with him in our control, they have no one to command them. Yes, my boy, you are safe."

Steven glanced at the wall clock and jumped up. "I have to get to bed before my aunt wakes up! She must never find out about any of this or she'll ground me for sure! For life!"

Bastet leaped from the table and followed Steven to the metal door of the windowless lab. "Thanks, Shu, again, for saving Bastet and me from the scorpions," Steven called over his shoulder. "Thank you, Seeker for everything."

The Seeker smiled. "I will return in three days to assist you in planning for our next trip. Get some rest."

Steven whirled around. "Another trip?" He shook his head. "I just can't wait to jump into the next heart-throbbing, bone-chilling, wonderful adventure."

The Seeker would have laughed, but there wasn't anything funny about the dangers he knew Steven might soon be facing.

Steven saw Bastet charge up the stairs ahead of him. That cat is getting stranger and stranger, he thought, as he pushed open the door that led to the kitchen. It seemed quiet until...

"Good morning Steven." His aunt surprised him as he walked into the kitchen. "You're up early?"

Steven froze. *What is she doing here?*

"How did you get so filthy?" Aunt Celia frowned.

"Oh, it's … just a little sand."

"You're covered in dust from head to toe." Her eyes studied him carefully.

Steven had to think fast. "Bastet and I went for a walk, along the river."

"A walk got you this filthy?" She eyed him with suspicion.

Steven knew he was about to get caught. "On the way back to the house, I tripped over a... a log. It was washed up from yesterday's storm. Remember the storm?"

Aunt Celia shook her head. "Did you fall in the desert? You look like you're covered in sand? You also look absolutely exhausted."

Steven let out a huge yawn. "I couldn't sleep. The storm was so bad. So, I went back to my parents' lab. I just sat around and read some more in Mom and Dad's journals."

"You've been up all night?" Aunt Celia frowned. "We'll talk about this later, young man. Right now, you'd better go up to your room, clean up, and get some sleep!"

Steven muttered an apology as he left the kitchen, relieved that she didn't notice his boots, flannel shirt, and Levies—not exactly summer beachwear. Someday, it wouldn't be so easy. Someday he might have to tell his aunt what he was really doing. The problem was, he wasn't sure himself.

Chapter 2

Drooling Slayer was breathing hard from pulling his huge weight through the lava tubes after leaving the Ruler's cavern. He and a dragon had been released from captivity to search for a small boy. The heat of the magma and the thick blanket of steam were draining his energy. The slick ground and jagged rock surface were causing him to slip and slide as he tried to pull himself forward. His leather tunic was soaked with sweat. He had to hunch over to keep from scraping his head against the rough ceiling of the cave, all not easy with his massive body only supported by two stubby legs ending in long flat feet that made it hard to run. "I hate climbing these rocks," he said, staring ahead at what looked like miles and miles of more rocks.

His hands, and long fingers, tipped with sharp claws, helped him climb up the slippery slopes, or he would never have made it. Sharp poisonous quills jutting from his arms and legs, made him look like a giant porcupine. His sweat, laced with a powerful acid, seeped from the many pores in his skin, making any enemy's eyes water. When the acidic drops fell to the limestone floor, they sizzled noisily, and made the smooth surfaces even more slippery. "I hate this climbing," Drooling Slayer repeated. "This hunt for a mortal, a boy yet, is a waste of my time and strength."

Flying ahead of the grumbling Slayer was Batena, a vampire bat. She was the Ruler's favorite scout, currently assigned to assist the Slayer in searching for the boy. She thought it would be very easy to satisfy her master and earn a generous reward. She didn't understand why the Slayer was so angry about being assigned such an easy mission. A mere boy would be no match for the might of this powerful and cruel hunter. "Wha' wrong wid you?" She squealed in Bat to the rotten-smelling beast.

The Slayer brandished his club in his hand, swinging it, as if he wanted to use it on something or someone. As he emerged from the lava tube, a growl rolled up from his throat.

Three Grool Hogs had unexpectedly appeared. Smaller than him, they looked surprisingly fearsome, with thick necks and leathery brown skin covered with spines. Most importantly, there were three of them.

The Slayer gasped. He remembered the day he'd first encountered these beasts. He had been searching for three days on Mt. Saint Helen, for food and a place to rest from the ferocious weather. The wind was howling, and the driving snow blinded him. Slipping on a patch of ice, he careened off the rocks and fell into a deep crevasse. Bruised and bleeding, he managed to pull himself up from the snow. As he looked around, he saw a cave in the side of the mountain behind him. Shelter, he thought.

Forcing his way through the snowdrift, he squeezed through the hollow. He sat in the dark trying to shake off the cold. When his eyes adjusted, he saw an opening into the mountain behind him. A smell like rotten eggs came from it. Food, he thought, and pushed his way into a narrow, dark, passageway. He crawled through what seemed to be an endless tunnel. His hands and knees were bleeding from the roughness of the walls. He thought of going back, but it was too tight to turn. He had no choice but to keep crawling ahead.

Finally, the passage opened just wide enough for him to stand. His head brushed against a colony of bats clinging to the ceiling.

The bats squealed and swooped down around him.

Feeling their wings and teeth on his skin, Slayer roared, wildly swinging his club at the hundreds of bats he had disturbed. Desperately fighting off the bats, he didn't notice three creatures lurking in the shadows.

It was the Grool Hogs.

Seeing him distracted by the swirling bats, the hungry hogs saw their advantage and attacked. They pummeled him with large clubs, targeting his head, until they forced him down on one knee.

Surprised by their attack, the far more powerful beast barely managed to maintain a grip on his club, swinging it in a desperate effort to defend himself.

The hogs kept up the beating. Their attack never let up.

The Slayer could hardly move in the tight area and soon was overcome by their constant blows. Exhausted, unable to rise, he closed his eyes and waited for the death blow.

It never came.

Instead, he was surprised to hear angry arguing among his three tormentors.

"Kill him, Krill," snorted a hog he would later know as Gos.

Krill lifted his club high, ready to deliver the fatal blow.

"No," another hog, Tol, shouted, jumping between Gos and their victim. "Do you want to be torn apart by the Ruler's pets? The Ruler told everyone to bring him back alive. Now, tie him up!"

"Easy for you to say," snapped Gos. "I have not eaten in three days!" He took a step toward Drooling Slayer. "I'll butcher him myself."

"Get back!" Tol ordered. He was the tallest of the three and planted his two flat feet firmly on the stone floor.

Drooling Slayer was recovering his strength. All he needed was a few more seconds and these stupid beasts would get quite a surprise. He was about to get up when a loud scream startled him.

Gos had lunged toward Tol, club held high.

Knowing this was probably his best opportunity to escape, Drooling Slayer slammed his club into the gut of the beast nearest him.

Krill, taken off guard, fell to the ground.

The Slayer pivoted and threw himself at Gos with the full weight of his huge body.

Gos was thrown against the tunnel wall. He cried out in agony as poisonous spines penetrated his chest.

Tol heard his brother's cry and charged the Slayer.

With lighting speed, Drooling Slayer swung at the hog. His club was deflected by Tol's, which slammed against his head. Stunned by the blow, Drooling Slayer swayed. Unable to maintain his balance, he tried to fend off a second, and then a third vicious blow. It was no use. The battered Slayer fell to the ground.

This time the hogs continued to beat him with their clubs until he was unconscious.

The Slayer did not know how long he slept, but after a good amount of time, opened his eyes. He realized he had been bound tightly and left in a dimly lit cavern. He shivered, recalling the battle. He'd never been defeated in a fight before. Fearing his enemies' return, he struggled to break free of his bonds and escape. But now there was something else holding him back.

Two piercing, red eyes were staring down at him.

The Slayer felt a chill race through his body. It was something he'd never felt before, a chill of fear. He tried again to pull free of the bonds, but they held him tight.

The eyes watched silently.

Finally, the Slayer stopped struggling. Too terrified to speak, he lay trembling on the stone floor. The evil emanating from the eyes had overwhelmed him.

That night he became a servant of the Ruler of Darkness. The memory of the Ruler's eyes as they had held him captive, made him shiver again. He remembered well that same icy glare when the Ruler had given him this assignment. His words had been spoken with chilling calm, "I want that boy. You shall search for the boy responsible for releasing The Seeker from my cell and then freeing the spirit of the Guardian of Seti I."

He remembered feeling as if the eyes were long pointy fingernails poking into his flesh, as the Ruler continued to speak, "Find that boy and bring him to me, alive, and you shall be rewarded." He could almost see the Ruler's eyes dig even deeper when he leaned forward and said, "If you fail to do my bidding, you will suffer punishment far beyond your worst fears."

The three hogs glared at the Slayer and went on their way. They knew he was one of them now, a slave of the Dark Ruler.

Batena stopped to eat a tiny rodent.

The Slayer thought of getting his revenge on the hogs. I do not want to risk being punished again, he reminded himself. "Get moving, you lazy bat," he growled, swinging his club at Batena, who smartly stayed just out of his reach. "What use is a puny bat in the capture of this boy?" he barked. I'll bet he sent this bat to spy on me, the Slayer thought. "You had better keep up then! Let's get this hunt over with!"

"Just remember, I am the Ruler's favorite. I am not the one who will get roasted and fed to the Hyenas if you fail. It is you who must hurry."

The Slayer thought of smashing the treacherous little bat's head to a pulpy mess with his club, but she was right, he needed her. "I'll take care of her later, but first we must find the boy."

The bat soared high into the air. The hunt was on.

* * * * * *

The Slayer trudged toward the entrance of another cavern. The sound of heavy breathing echoed off the walls. The silhouette of a dragon lay against the back wall. Drooling Slayer walked toward the pool of black stagnant water. She was still here. He smiled at the sight of the gigantic body. He walked over where she lay and kicked the steel chains holding her captive.

Morag opened her right eye. Her face showed her fear.

The sound of slurping was heard as Batena drew blood from the dragon's neck.

"You will obey me," Drooling Slayer growled, his club raised, eyes searching for smoke streaming from her nostrils.

The dragon lifted her head and nodded sadly.

10

Drooling Slayer jumped upon the back of Morag. He released the chains from the massive collar around her neck. "I am your master," he said, and struck his club in warning on his captive's side. "Should you fail to obey me, you shall suffer torment worse than your worst nightmares." He deliberately used the Dark Ruler's own words, words that terrified even his soul. "Fly! Fly," the Slayer commanded.

Batena clung to Morag's scale under her neck. No reason to waist my energy, she thought.

The dragon ran toward the edge of the cliff and flapping its massive wings, launched herself into the sky. Someday soon, she swore, she would again be free.

A kick on her side told her to head East.

The Slayer knew that if he relaxed even for one instant, the dragon might try to hurl him off her back. He also knew that his keeping her chained in the dark cave had proven to her he was her master. Yes, he thought, feeling the amazing sense of power that came from flying on her back, the intoxicating sensation of flying in the sky. "Someday I will be free of the Dark Ruler and will use this beast to control the world. But for now, we head to Egypt where we shall begin our hunt for that boy." He smiled, thinking of what the Dark Ruler was going to do to that miserable boy once he was captured. I wouldn't want to be that boy for all the gold in the world, he thought, as the clouds passed below the dragon's powerful wings. "Boy," he screamed, "You haven't got a chance!"

Chapter 3

Steven rushed to open the door, his eyes glowing with excitement.

"Happy 13th Birthday!" his friends, shouted.

"Thank you! Come on in!"

"Hello, boys." Aunt Celia smiled. "Come into the kitchen and get your soda and snacks. But don't get too comfortable. The party is in the dining room in the North Wing."

Steven stared after his aunt. He had not been in the North Wing since his parents died. He followed his friends into the kitchen where they each grabbed a can of soda.

"Follow me, boys," Aunt Celia said, leading them out of the kitchen and down the hall to the pair of carved wooden doors.

Am I ready to go in there? Steven wondered.

"I've never been in this part of your house before," Paul said. "Come to think of it, I've never been anywhere in your house before."

"Me neither," Charlie said.

Steven smiled uneasily.

"Enter if you dare," Aunt Celia said, pulling on the bronze door handles. The doors opened with an eerie scraping sound.

"Awesome!" Scotty exclaimed, seeing the long table full of goodies in the center of the room.

Steven bit his lip, remembering the last time he'd entered this room. It had been his last dinner with his parents before they left for Egypt. "Cool," Charlie said, "It sounds like a haunted house on T.V.."

Steven felt a warm breeze against his cheek. "Shu? Are you here?"

he whispered, thinking it had to be the Egyptian wind god returning from one of his long trips across the world.

"Shoe?" Rusty asked. "Is there something wrong with your shoe?"

"What? My shoe? No. Nothing." Steven realized he had to stay focused. How could he explain about the God of Wind to his friends? They would never believe any of his story anyway. *Stay focused.*

The boys, peering into the room, hesitated at the door.

Steven wondered what made them not enter. He knew what was keeping him out.

"Come on, boys," Aunt Celia coaxed. "There's nothing to be afraid of."

As they entered, Aunt Celia turned off the hallway lights, plunging them into near darkness. She'd always been a bit of a ham and wanted to give Steven a very special birthday. "Welcome mortals," Aunt Celia hissed in a ghostly voice, and then, without warning, hurried back down the hallway. "I'll be back...if you are still here?" She let out another evil laugh and disappeared.

"What are you all waiting for?" Rusty asked, groping the wall for a light switch. He found the switch next to the door frame. "Come on, Steven, what's wrong with you? You going to miss your own party?"

"Hey, Steven, your aunt made you a fantastic party. She's somethin' else!" Paul laughed.

Steven's friends were all laughing, but he hardly heard them. He was staring at the red leather couch near the fireplace. He saw his parents seated on the couch. He was seated between them. They were holding a scrapbook and showing him their photos of their last trip to Egypt. He remembered feeling a chill, wishing they wouldn't go back to the tombs again. Why didn't he tell them what he was sensing? Why didn't he stop them?

Aunt Celia returned carrying a large white frosted cake.

"Hey Steven, get a load of this great cake!"

Steven turned away from the couch at the sound of his name. He didn't want to stay here. He felt guilty he hadn't stopped his parents...he had never told anyone that he knew they were not coming back. He hadn't even told them how much he loved them. "I want to go back," he said too softly for the others to hear, not wanting them to see his eyes.

"What does it say, Steven?" asked Paul.

"It says, You're the Best," Scotty said.

"Aunt Celia, you are so cool!" said Rusty.

"Start opening your presents!" Paul shouted.

"Mine first," yelled Rusty. "It's the one in white paper."

Steven was still standing away from the table. He saw the big smile on his aunt's face and realized she couldn't possibly know what he was feeling. He glanced at the others. They definitely didn't know. He turned back to the couch. There was no one there. They'd never be there again. He let out a deep sigh. If they were here, would they want him to ruin the party? He gave his aunt a smile and sat down in front of the pile of gifts. "Is this the first one?" he asked.

"Open it," Aunt Celia said still smiling.

Steven saw the smile but couldn't return it. He unwrapped Rusty's present. It was a thick book, *"The Stand*, by Steven King. Thanks, Rusty," he said, thinking how the great horror writer would have a field day writing about his incredible adventures.

Paul's gift was next. It was a book called, *Gods of Egyptian Mythology*. *How did Paul know to buy that?* "Thanks, Paul. I love mythology."

Paul shrugged. "I just saw it in the store, and it was like calling me to buy it. It was weird, like you, Steven."

Aunt Celia smiled. "Great gift, Paul. It fits right in with my nephew's summer assignment."

Steven wondered if she believed his lie. He also wondered what made Paul buy that particular book.

Scotty's gift was next.

Steven shook it. "Another book?" He removed the last of the wrapper and read the title, *The Town below the Ground*.

Scotty shrugged. "For our class trip to Scotland, in three weeks. Did you forget?"

With all his adventures in Egypt, how could he even think of Scotland?

"What's it about?" Rusty asked, thinking he'd be disappointed if all he got was a bunch of books for his birthday. Steven was different. That's for sure.

Scotty shrugged again. "I think it's about this hidden metropolis under Edinburgh. I never read it. I don't even know what made me buy it. It was just there."

Steven studied the cover. "I think it'll be interesting to read before we get there. I like it. Thanks, Scott," he said, flipping through the pages.

Aunt Celia still wasn't sure she loved the idea of Steven going to Scotland, even on a class trip. She had decided to allow it in the hope it might help take his mind off what happened to his parents. There were too many times when she had caught him looking sadly out the window, almost as if he expected them to come back. That's why she had decided to go with him.

Steven reached for Charlie's present next, not knowing what to expect from the prankster. A gag gift would be a welcome change with all the reading he had to finish. He placed the small rectangular box close to his ear and shook it.

"You'll never guess," Charlie crowed. "And no hints you guys!"

Steven tore at the wrapping paper and slid out a red box with a picture of the 'goliath' of Swiss Army knives on the lid.

"You should have all the tools you'll ever need in that baby," Charlie bragged. "It's the best gift ever!"

"Awesome! Thanks!" Steven examined the knife. The blade was sharp. He pulled out the other tools. "This will come in very handy," he said, wishing he could tell them exactly for what, but knowing if he included them, their lives would be at risk too.

"The idea came to me in a dream I had about you," Charlie said. "It was a strange dream. You were in a cave—"

An alarm went off in Steven's brain. He cut him off. "You're crazy, Charlie. Great gift though."

Charlie, shrugged. Maybe later he'd tell Steven about his strange dream.

Steven didn't want the others to hear Charlie's dream. He didn't want to hear it either.

"It's time for my present, Steven."

Steven turned to his aunt. "You didn't have to give me anything. This party with my friends is plenty."

"I do have to give you this." Aunt Celia handed him a large envelope.

He ripped open the envelope and silently read the handwritten note inside.

Dear Steven,

I am sad at what brought us together as a family but overjoyed at having been chosen by your parents to be your guardian. I love you as if you were my own son and will never forget the opportunity I have been given to help raise such a wonderful, intelligent, young man.

Always with love,

Aunt Celia

Steven folded the card back into the envelope. He could hardly speak. "Thank you, Aunt Celia."

"Was it money?" Rusty asked.

"Better," Steven replied.

Aunt Celia sensed his embarrassment. "Come on now, open your other gift," she said, hoping Steven liked what she had written on his card. She knew she could never take the place of his parents, but she wanted him to know that she truly cared about him. She wondered if he'd ever fully understand that.

Steven tucked the card into his jeans pocket. He didn't want to show any emotion in front of the others, so he grabbed the box and tore off the paper.

"All RIGHT!" Charlie said. "Great gift! I wish I had an aunt like you!"

"A new smart phone?" Rusty exploded. "That's the best on the market."

"Cool," shouted Paul. "You got the latest one! Can I see it?"

Steven handed him the phone. He watched as the other boys examined its features.

His aunt was beaming with joy. "Do you like your gift?" she asked.

"I like them both." He gave her a warm smile and squeezed her hand. "Thank you."

Aunt Celia wished she could hug him, but she understood that would take time. For now, this was enough. Still holding his hand, she said, "Time for cake and ice cream, boys!" She let go of his hand and handed him the cake knife. "You do the honors."

"Well, now that the food's over, what do we do now?" Rusty asked.

Steven said, "I have a surprise gift for all of you down in the lab."

His aunt looked surprised. What had he cooked up for them?

She thought about not letting him go, but realized showing off his parents' lab...now, his lab, might help him feel better about himself. "I'll start cleaning up," she said, never thinking there could be anything dangerous about Steven bringing the boys down to the basement laboratory. "Go, have fun with your friends."

Steven imagined the expressions on their faces once the 'action' started. It had taken a while to convince The Seeker to help. "Steven, this is not an entertainment," he had said, but finally gave in. Tonight, his friends would experience the same kind of thrills and chills he had on his quest to find The Guardian of the Tomb in ancient Egypt. They would think it was a game. He would be the only one who would know it was all too real.

Chapter 4

Steven pulled open the door and entered the lab. Rusty followed quickly behind him. Scotty wanted to peer in without entering, but Rusty yanked him inside. Charlie brought up the rear, reluctant to remain in the dark hallway. Steven flipped on the switch, flooding the lab with white fluorescent light.

"Whoa!" Scotty exclaimed, "Is this all yours?

All the boys were astonished by the number of books stacked along the walls, tables, and floor. They gaped at the tools used by Steven's parents, now piled up in one of the corners. Large albums, filled with photos of various archeological sites were resting on shelves stationed around the room, and maps of explorations his parents had gone on, were posted on the walls.

"This place is cool," Paul said, examining book titles on the floor.

"It's just 'his 'parents' laboratory," Rusty muttered, a bit jealous.

"I'd be living in this room if this was my house," Paul said.

"Oh, yuck! Look at this!"

Everyone turned to Scotty, who was holding up a jar. "Doesn't this thing look gross?"

Steven said softly, "It's a mummified cat, Scotty."

Scotty looked closer and shivered. "Working in a room full of mummified animals would give me the creeps."

"This is even cooler," Rusty shouted from the other side of the room. "This jar has eyeballs in it!" He held it in front of Scotty's eyes. "Here's looking at you, Scotty!" He let out a laugh when the smaller boy backed up.

"I have heard of pickled eggs before, but not pickled eyes," Paul said with a shiver.

"They always give me the creeps too." Steven took the jar from Rusty. "You shouldn't touch this stuff. It's all rare."

"What are these chairs set up for?" Rusty asked, walking over to a group of chairs placed in a semi-circle.

"This is the entertainment I promised you guys. I've put together videos from some of my parents' expeditions in Egypt. I made up sort of an adventure game for you."

"Awesome!" Charley exclaimed, rushing to the chairs.

Rusty grabbed the viewer hanging over the back of a chair and sat down. "Probably a bore, but let's get it over with."

Steven turned off the overhead lights. "Go ahead and put on your viewers. Tell me when you're ready."

The others scrambled to the chairs and pulled the viewers over their heads.

Steven adjusted his eyepieces and announced in his most dramatic voice, "Get ready for 'Adventure in the Tomb of Seti I'!"

"What's Seti I?" Rusty asked.

Steven announced, "The place: the Valley of the Kings in Egypt!" He clicked on the 'Seti I' icon on his computer screen. He couldn't wait for the fun to begin. But suddenly, he remembered it hadn't been fun. It had been terrifying dealing with the Dark Ruler's monsters while searching the pyramid for the tomb of the Guardian they were protecting. This is a mistake, he thought, but it was too late. The program had begun. They were all looking at a wall covered with hieroglyphs. "You are in the tomb of Seti I," Steven announced.

"It looks real," Charlie said, thinking he had the coolest best friend ever.

Scotty was a little anxious. This looked too real for him.

"It looks fake to me," Rusty muttered.

As the boys were staring into their viewers, The Seeker materialized next to the back wall. He studied each boy with interest. They were the first boys, except for Steven, that he had seen in centuries. They are much like Steven, and yet they are not, he thought. We shall see. He rose into the air and moved silently behind them, sprinkling a bit of fine powder over each of their heads.

"Did you feel something soft land on your head?" Scotty asked, looking up.

Rusty touched his hair, but he didn't want to sound worried. "You're just imagining it," he said.

"Steven, is this your aunt's trick? I felt something too." Charley muttered.

"Don't worry," Steven said, "It's part of the show."

The Seeker, with a wave of his hand, took control of the images and sounds they were seeing. The image of the interior of the tomb's chamber became even more real, now in his version of 3D.

"Cool!" Charley said. "This is like being in a 3D movie. Steven, this is really cool!"

Rusty ran his hand through his hair again. Something strange was happening.

Steven still thought he was controlling the virtual reality experience. But why did the images seem so real?

There was a sudden burst of bright light and the boys were surprised to see themselves on screen, walking to the end of the chamber. "Hey Steven, is that you?"

"How are you doing that, Steven?" Charlie asked. "That's me up there!"

Paul mumbled. "I don't like this dark place."

"It's just a fake tunnel," Rusty spat, but he had to admit there was something spooky about all this.

Steven didn't reply. The images on the walls of the passageway weren't what he'd programmed. *The Seeker!* Had The Seeker added special 'stuff' to the video to make it a little more 'fun' for his friends? That's what he'd wanted. He had asked The Seeker to let his friends experience only a little of what he had seen in the pyramid. It was supposed to be a little, harmless, prank…

Steven heard heavy breathing near the figure that he recognized as himself. He leaned forward, listening to what sounded like shoes scraping along the sand-covered stone floor in the narrow tunnel. He felt strange, as if the air had changed. It was difficult to breathe. It was cold. His heart was pounding. "No, it can't be," Steven's brain said. He moved his joystick to make his avatar touch the wall. *OMG! It felt real. It is real.* "I can't be back here. Seeker, I didn't mean for us to actually go back." He tried to pull off the viewer, but it wouldn't budge.

Charlie gripped his chair. "Steven, what's happening? I can't see where I'm going!"

"The air in here smells gross," Paul said.

"It's all fake," Rusty replied, but felt the choking sensation himself.

Steven didn't answer. There was something wrong. "This is not what I wanted. Seeker, what are you up to?"

You will soon find out, Steven, The Seeker thought, waving his arm again.

A gray beam of light pierced the darkness.

"This is so cool," Rusty said, but was feeling anxious. It seemed too real to be a movie, so what was it?

"There's more drawings on the walls," Scotty said as his avatar stretched to see the drawings.

Steven could barely make out the inscriptions on the walls as The Seeker moved their avatars down another long, sand-filled corridor.

"This is boring. Let's find the exit," Rusty ordered, believing he was in command of this virtual tour.

Steven wished he could lead them to an exit. Two beams of light sweeping the walls ahead put that thought to the back of his head. As he got closer, he realized the beams were coming from two flashlights. He walked closer. He heard voices. They were muffled, but he could make out their conversation:

"Before we head back to the surface, let's try the passageway to your left."

"I think we should leave," a woman replied. "Our batteries are almost dead."

"We have time," the man said.

"These voices sound familiar! Who are these people?" Steven strained to see the strangers' faces in the shadows of the corridor. He was still too far, and the room was too dark.

"We'll have enough light to complete our initial search of these tunnels before we head back," the man said.

"I hope you're right. I wouldn't want to grope around in this tomb trying to find our way out in the dark," the woman responded.

"Mother? That sounds like my mother's voice. But it can't be. She died... Seeker, where are you?" Steven tried to pull off the viewer again, but it still wouldn't come off. I don't want to see this.

The two flashlight beams continued to move down the long, narrow passageway.

Steven saw his friends were now following the flashlight beams. "Seeker, what are you doing? I know I'm still in my parents' lab. This is just a video, but it's too real. It feels like I'm in that tomb again. Who is that couple? Are they my parents?" he said telepathically. Steven touched the wall with his palm and yanked it back. "I touched it," he said aloud, having felt cold stone. He inhaled and smelled the musty odor of the tomb. "This is real! My friends! Where are they?"

The boys were still moving ahead of him, a small procession, down the corridor.

"This isn't scary at all, Steven," Rusty said, but wondered what the two people in front of his avatar were up to. He didn't want to show he was afraid, but this was too real-feeling.

"I want to go back," Paul muttered.

"You're just a chicken," Rusty replied, but wished the video, or whatever it was, would stop and they'd find themselves back in the lab. Even with all the crazy things in that windowless room, it was less scary than this dark tomb they were now exploring with two shadowy strangers leading them to who knows where? "It's just V.R.," he said, but knew it was like no virtual reality game he'd ever played before.

Steven's face brushed up against thick spider webs. They clung tightly around his face and neck as he tried to back away. Something crawled down his collar. He slapped his hand against his flesh. Got it, he thought, pulling the sticky web off his face.

Scotty yelled, "I hate spider webs! Steven, what are you doing to us? It feels sticky!" He pulled at the web sticking to his hair.

Steven now realized the others were experiencing what he was going through. Did they see the man and woman too?

Suddenly, the man shouted, "Let's go! We have to get out of here! My lamp is going out!"

Chapter 5

The woman's lantern flickered. "I told you so," she muttered. "Make sure the cover is still tight."

Steven's mother twisted the cover. The lights shown bright.

"Hurry! Keep up!" The man shouted over his shoulder. "You boys must keep up with us if you expect to get out alive!"

"Alive?" Charlie yelled. "What does he mean, Steven?"

"This isn't real, Steven. Is it?" Even Rusty was worried now.

"I don't know," Steven said, "but we'd better do as Dad says. Stay close. Don't take chances!"

"That's your father?" Charlie asked, wondering what the heck was happening.

The boys followed as fast as they could, trying not to crash into each other in the narrow tunnel.

Steven guarded the rear. He was furious at The Seeker. "What am I doing here, Seeker? My friends think that I'm in control of all this! Boy, are they wrong! You're scaring them. You're scaring me!" he voiced his concern telepathically. "Guys keep going," Steven shouted over the boys' anxious jabbering.

"I don't like this anymore," Paul whined.

Neither do I, Steven thought, promising he would have a long talk with The Seeker when the 'joke' was over.

His parents stopped walking.

Steven crashed into Rusty, knocking him onto the sandy floor.

"What the? Steven! Are you crazy?" Rusty shouted, picking himself up off the floor. "What are you doing? Shut this thing off! It isn't fun anymore. You're scaring Paul!"

Steven didn't reply. He was staring at the wall. A chill raced to his brain when he recognized the carving. He saw the crocodile jaws open wide.

"It's a Devourer," his father said, pointing to the image. "It's one of the most vicious creatures in Egyptian mythology. The legends say they were sealed in these tombs to protect the dead Pharaohs and their riches." He ran his finger over the outline.

"Pretty hideous, if you ask me," his mother replied. "I'm glad they're only myths."

Steven, staring at the monstrous figure, thought he noticed it move. He blinked his eyes, thinking it was his imagination, but the carving slowly turned her head toward him, drool dripping from her lips.

The long snout of the beast was pulling free from the craggy wall.

Steven shouted, "It's alive!"

Steven's father backed away. "Let's get out of here!"

His mother was staring at the wall as if hypnotized.

"I said, let's go!" Steven's father grabbed her wrist and pulled her with him.

Steven saw the others running after his parents.

The Devourer's head and neck were now breaking free of the stone wall. Soon it would be completely free.

Steven, stunned by the horrifying apparition, seemed unable to move. Suddenly he felt a hand wrap around his fingers. "Mom?" She was dragging him down the passageway. "Mom? Is it really you?" A shrill roar reminded him of the danger to his friends. "Where are the others?"

"They're safe, Steven," his mother said. "But you're not."

"But the beast. It isn't real. Is it?" Steven turned, terrified to see the Devourer about to attack, but she was nowhere in sight. The beam of his light revealed she had returned to her prison, trapped as a carving in the stone. "I don't understand," he muttered. "I don't understand any of this."

"You will, son." Steven's mother said, still holding his hand guiding him forward in the dark tunnel.

He had so many questions for his mother, but now saw his dad had stopped again. "What is he looking at?" Steven saw his father was examining a picture painted on the wall inches above the floor.

"The Guardian is here somewhere," his father said in a strained voice. "We've got to find him."

"He shouldn't do that," Steven said, but his mother was no longer with him. "Now where did she go?" *he* asked.

His father was bent down, scratching the limestone out of two concealed holes in the upper corners of the slab.

Steven felt his mother again standing next to him. "What are you doing?" Steven's mom yanked on his father's jacket. "We can't stay here. It's too dangerous."

"I've got to know if this is the Guardian's resting place," Steven's father said. "You know the prophecy." He looked back at Steven.

The prophecy? Steven wondered if his father was referring to the same prophecy that had been revealed to him by The Seeker. Did his parents know about it? Had they always known?

His mother shot the flashlight beam around the cave-like walls. "The Devourer is near. We've got to get Steven out of here now." She peered anxiously down the tunnels.

"Not yet. We have time. Have one of the boys keep watch while I enter the vault. If the Guardian is there maybe I can destroy it and end the danger for our son. I've got to try."

"No Dad," Steven shouted, "It's too dangerous." He was beginning to understand what he was seeing. "Don't do this for me! I need you."

"I have to try and save you, Steven," his father said, pulling on the stone.

The slab swung open, revealing a passageway.

Steven watched helplessly as his father stepped through. He tried to hold onto his mother, but she followed.

"Rusty, please stand guard."

"If you think I am standing out here alone, your nuts!"

Steven shivered. Was any of this real? It felt as if it was. He hesitated at the entrance, but knew he had to do something when he saw his friends enter the same chamber into which his parents had disappeared. Were they in danger? How could he know since he was no longer in control? Without thinking of his own safety, he rushed inside.

In the dim light, Steven saw they were all standing around a large wooden box in the center of the chamber.

"Steven. You shouldn't be here," his mother said. "Go now. We'll protect you."

Steven wanted to leave, but saw Charlie, Rusty, Scotty, and Paul were huddled together against the wall.

"Something stinks," said Paul, his voice echoing in the tomb.

"I smell it, too," Scotty said. "It's like super-B.O.!"

Steven turned in time to see his father and mother pulling at the lid of the coffin. "No," he screamed, remembering how their contact with the mummy had led to their death.

'CRASH!'

Chapter 6

"Holy cow! What was that?" Rusty shouted.

Steven heard it too. The lid had crashed to the ground.

"There's a mummy in here," Steven's father said. "It must be the Guardian."

The chamber became quiet, dead quiet. No one moved.

Then Steven saw his friends inch their way to the coffin. "Keep away from it. It killed them. It will kill you."

"We have to do this for our son's sake," his father said, grabbing the canvas covering and pulling it away.

There was a blood-curdling scream.

"Paul, your scream scared the hell out of us," Rusty said, staring at the most hideous face he'd ever seen.

"Look at him," Paul said, covering his eyes. "No wonder he stinks. He's gross!"

"Quiet," Steven's father ordered, as he bent over the coffin.

"Stop Dad. Please?" Steven didn't want to look. He could picture the Guardian's face, leathery skin stretched taut over the skull; a mouth stretched wide, as if screaming in terror. "It's one of them!" He'd seen this grotesque face before and had hoped never to see it again. "Seeker stop it! Stop it now!" Why was The Seeker doing this? He was supposed to be Steven's friend. "I said stop it!" Steven shouted. He heard a strange noise and turned back to the scene by the coffin.

He saw his father touch the Guardian's bindings and become transfixed by the skeleton face. It's too late, he thought, staring helplessly and knowing what was going to happen next.

A low snarling sound came from the mummy's gaping mouth.

Steven, in a daze, walked toward the coffin. Taking a deep breath, he looked down.

The hollow eye sockets began to glow.

Steven pulled at his father's sleeve, but it was as if he were grasping at air. "Come on, guys, we've got to go. Please? Let's go?"

His friends were too afraid to move.

The eyes were now blazing fireballs.

"Look at that," Steven heard a voice say.

The two orbs were now the eyes of a massive snake. It was weaving before him, its mouth opening, exposing two long fangs. Its tongue darted toward him.

"Back away slowly," Steven said. "Rusty, move very slowly along the wall."

The boys were transfixed by the snake's eyes.

"Walk away. Rusty! Snap out of it!" Steven punched him hard on his arm.

Rusty shouted, "What the heck? That is one gigundo snake!" He backed away. "Uh, guys? Guys, back up really slowly."

The boys tried to back away, but they couldn't move.

The head weaved closer, studying each of their faces. It was as if it was deciding which boy to attack first.

"No!" Steven erupted, "You can't have my friends!" He hissed to the others. "He's here for me. The Guardian has transformed into this snake because he wants me."

"You're nuts," Rusty said, trying to keep his leadership role. "This is just a trick. It's just a video game... Isn't it?"

The snake roared and Rusty jumped.

Steven pushed Rusty back. "Who are you? What do you want?"

The snake hissed, "So, you mortals dare to enter my sacred chamber?" He rose even higher.

The walls and ceiling of the room shook from his rage. Sand fell from the ceiling.

The snake paused, sniffing the air. "The boy? Which of you insignificant beings is the boy?"

Steven's mind was racing: *He doesn't know who I am. Do I tell him? Do I sacrifice myself for my friends? Will he leave them alone once he has me?*

The snake stopped weaving. "I sense someone 'special' is here," he hissed. "Yes, you are here." He let out a hellish laugh. "Tell me which of you is the boy from the prophecy and I shall let the others leave."

The others looked confused, frightened.

The snake sighed. "Very well. Such a feast I will have on your flesh and bones."

"Steven, this is really funny," Rusty said, but wished the video would stop.

"You think this is humorous, mortal?" The snake let his voice get louder, and louder in the death chamber.

Rusty covered his ears.

They all did.

"Prepare to meet your doom, mortals!" the snake hissed.

Steven shouted, "Guys, this isn't a game! We have to get out of here now!"

The snake's weaving motion still held the others in its spell. "So, you won't tell me which of you is the boy I seek? Very well. I shall kill all of you, one at a time, in the most delightfully painful way." He prepared to launch his fangs into Scotty who was the nearest.

Chapter 7

Steven was about to announce to the snake that he was the boy from the prophecy when he heard his father's voice. "I am the one you seek, you monster. I am the mortal of the prophecy."

Before Steven could reply, he heard a loud roar from the snake and saw the head lunge toward his father.

"Dad, save yourself!" Steven shouted.

His father smiled sadly. "No, Steven, I must save you."

The snake struck quickly, its huge body blocking Steven's view.

There was a terrible scream.

Steven's mother caught his father as he fell to the ground.

Rusty held Steven, keeping him from running to his father.

"Good-bye, son. Always remember, we did this because we love you."

The snake hissed and struck again.

A female's agonized scream echoed in the chamber.

"It was all for you," his mother said. "Always remember, it was all for you."

Steven let out a scream when he saw the image burst into millions of flashing stars.

Then the room was black.

They're gone. They're both gone. Steven searched the blackness but knew he would never see his parents again. He felt angry, his hands formed into tight fists. He wished he could smash something, anything, to stop him from crying. Nothing helped. He wiped teardrops from his eyes, hoping the others didn't see them.

"They sacrificed themselves for you," Steven, a voice said softly as the smoke cleared and Steven found himself back in the outer chamber of the pyramid with The Seeker. "That is what they asked me to show you. They wanted me to show you they did it because they love you. It was their special birthday present to you."

"Birthday present? What kind of present is this?" He glared at The Seeker.

The Seeker sighed. "They wanted you to know they gave up their lives to try and keep you safe."

Steven couldn't stop the tears from flowing down his face. "They failed. They didn't save me. They didn't stop the prophecy. I still have to fight the Guardians and the Dark Ruler. They died for nothing...for nothing."

The Seeker gave him a fatherly smile. "That's not true. You know it's not true. They knew they had to die or you would die. They want you to understand that you are the most important thing in their lives. They want you to know how much they loved you...still love you."

Steven was about to shout he'd never understand, but The Seeker was gone. "Sure, leave me like everyone else." He sank to the floor. "How did this happen? I just wanted to have some fun with my friends—scare them a little." He stared at the pit. "Mom, Dad, I caused your death...and now my friends are gone."

There was no answer.

"I'm sorry. I never should have tried to trick them—"

There was a flash of light.

Steven could see black and white spots popping in front of him. He raised his hands to his face, lifted the viewer off his eyes. "What are you doing here? I thought—"

"Steven," said Rusty still shivering in his chair. "We've got to turn this video of yours into a game. We could make millions."

"My throat is sore from screaming," said Scotty. "I actually felt as if I was in that tomb."

Steven shook his head. "Had it all been a joke? It had to have been 'him'. But why? Why would he do this to me?"

The Seeker materialized and waved his arm.

The boys were frozen in time.

Steven was furious. "You! Why did you play such a dirty trick on me?"

The Seeker frowned. "Do you forget it was your idea?"

"It wasn't my idea! It was dangerous! You could have hurt my friends..." Steven gazed at his friends, all frozen under the wizard's spell. "It was my idea." He let out a deep sigh. "I remember now."

The Seeker nodded. "I had to show you that what we are engaged in is not a joke, nor a game, dear Steven."

Steven stared at The Seeker, anger still seething inside him. "I thought we were friends," he said.

The Seeker sighed. "You wanted to frighten your friends. You risked revealing our ancient secrets to amuse yourself. I had to teach you to take our task seriously."

Steven sighed. "This happened because I wanted to scare my friends. I didn't think that I might hurt them. You're right. You made me see that scaring my best buds wasn't such a great idea." He had a bitter taste in his mouth. "How can I make it up to them?"

The Seeker smiled. "When I first met you, I didn't believe you could ever become the boy of the prophecy. You had so much to learn."

"And now?"

"You still have much to learn."

"I guess." Steven felt discouraged. "Will I ever learn?"

"If you wish it, you will learn."

"With lessons like this one?" Steven asked, shivering at how he felt when he thought all his friends had been left in the tomb with that snake-creature.

"Sometimes, I guess it is necessary to learn the hard way," The Seeker replied, "But you are a caring and bright boy, and most lessons you will learn on your own. This one, you had to experience to fully understand how sometimes, even when we don't mean to, we can hurt others, even put them in danger."

Steven got up. "I'll apologize right now."

"There is no need."

"Sure, there is. I was wrong."

"Yes, you were, but they will remember nothing of this. I have erased their memory. There is too much at stake if they remember what they witnessed. Imagine what the Dark Ruler would do with them to obtain their knowledge. No, it is best they do not remember anything of their adventure."

"I didn't think of that. You're right. I wouldn't want anyone to have to go through what I've been through."

"Go now. Enjoy your birthday with your friends while you can. Soon, we will have another mission, and you must be ready."

Steven nodded. "Thank you," he said softly.

The Seeker smiled. "Your parents loved you. That much you can believe."

Steven watched silently as The Seeker vanished in a mist of smoke. He still wasn't sure if he should be angry with his mentor but realized he had brought this hard lesson on himself.

He stood, shaking off the anxiety he felt and headed for the kitchen.

Noises were coming from the kitchen.

"Where have you been?" Rusty asked, holding a can of soda. "How does a birthday boy miss his own party?"

"You wouldn't believe it if I told you," Steven said, grabbing a can of soda and feeling grateful that his friends were all safe and gobbling up left-over pizza.

Steven thought how last year they'd sat around and told each other scary stories, watched TV, and stayed up late. This year he knew they'd been scared by a master—The Seeker.

Paul let out a loud yawn.

"I don't know why I'm so tired," Rusty said.

"I feel like I ran miles," Scotty added.

"And where'd all this sand come from?" Charlie asked, pulling sand from his belly button.

Steven thought everyone looked exhausted. Only he knew why.

Later that evening, as they lay in their bedrolls, each boy surrendered to sleep faster than they would have wanted.

Steven was the last to close his eyes. It was difficult to fall asleep knowing that what he had experienced today could become reality at any time. He wished he could forget too, but there were storm clouds swirling outside. Were they coming for him?

Chapter 8

After everyone left, Steven and his aunt went upstairs to clean his room. "Oh, my goodness!" she exclaimed after the light went on and Aunt Celia saw the mess from the party.

Steven had left his window open and a breeze was blowing the feathers around the room from a pillow fight the boys had when they woke up. He dashed to the window and closed it. Turning to face his aunt, he watched one feather float down and land right on the end of her nose. He waited for the explosion he deserved for the mess.

Aunt Celia looked at herself in the mirror, the feather on her nose. It stubbornly insisted on staying there. She shook her head and tossed a handful of feathers at Steven.

Steven laughed and threw feathers back at her. For a few minutes, he forgot all the dangers and problems he had been facing.

"Okay, enough," Aunt Celia finally said. "What a fun birthday party you had!" She began to collect the feathers.

"You don't know the half of it," murmured Steven, jumping down to help her.

Once the room was reasonably clean, Aunt Celia and Steven went down to the kitchen for lunch.

Steven was feeling relaxed until Aunt Celia said she had to go out, and added, "So keep out of mischief."

"Who me?"

Steven went to the lab wondering just what 'mischief' the next quest would involve. The Seeker had said they would be using the portal to teleport to Scotland.

"Why Scotland?" Steven asked as The Seeker materialized. "I don't know much about this amazing land."

The Seeker frowned. "We must free the Guardian of the Tomb in Glen Coe."

"Not another one?" Steven shivered. "Is he as bad as the last guy?"

"I fear worse. The Guardian is responsible for the massacre of Clan MacDonald. His name was Robert Campbell. During a cold winter night, Campbell led a group of English soldiers in killing the MacDonalds while they slept. The Ruler has placed Campbell guarding the mountains of Scotland waiting for the return of the MacDonalds," The Seeker said.

Booting up the computer, Steven doubled-clicked the Google Earth icon, which Steven had used to locate their arrival location in Egypt. Once Steven found a map of Scotland, he located Glen Coe. "Do you know where Campbell and his troops are hiding?" asked Steven. "The Scottish Highlands are a vast range of mountains."

"Ben Nevis, from what Shu has told me," said The Seeker.

"And what else has the Wind God told you?" Steven asked.

"He has noticed a number of hikers falling from the cliffs to their deaths from the north side of the mountain."

"And you think this is the Guardian's work?"

"I'm afraid so."

"You're immortal. You don't have to be afraid." Steven let out a deep sigh.

The Seeker decided to change the subject. "Well, Steven, did you enjoy my birthday gift?" The Seeker asked, brushing dust off his robe.

Steven shook his head. "Yeah! About as much as having liver for dinner."

"I'm glad. I always enjoyed eating calves' liver."

"I was being sarcastic," Steven replied.

"I see! You said that you wanted to have fun by scaring your friends. Didn't you?"

"Well, yes, but…"

"But what? I thought—"

"It was so real. We all freaked out! I felt as if I was back in the tomb fighting for my life."

The Seeker shook his head. "Yes. Perhaps now you understand the potential consequences before you decide to scare your friends again."

Steven didn't want another lecture. "I think we should get started on our quest to free the Guardian of the Tomb – Glen Coe you said?"

The Seeker hoped the boy had learned that these missions had to be taken seriously and had to be kept secret. "Have you located an entrance to the tomb yet?"

"Yes I found it."

"Good. Did your parents leave any notes describing their visit to the site last year?"

"I'll look through the journals and computer files," said Steven.

"Good! I will return tomorrow so be prepared."

The Seeker vanished before Steven could reply. "I can see why my parents had research assistants. I feel like one. This is my second assignment in three weeks!" He gave Bastet an angry look. "I should be watching TV, riding my bike, going to the beach, or sleeping-in, not chasing spirits and demons and whatever vicious, drooling thing wanders by to gobble me up."

Bastet raised her head and mewed.

Steven rubbed her back. "I suppose sitting here feeling sorry for myself and whining won't help." He let out a deep sigh. "I agreed to this quest. What choice did I have? That darn prophecy!"

Bastet stretched and mewed again.

Steven wondered how much she understood. "Hey, Bastet, it's not every kid that gets to travel anywhere in the world they want. I just wish it was a little less exciting." He walked to the bookcase and searched for a notebook labeled, Glen Coe. He found two composition notebooks on the lower shelf.

His parents' computer table was a semi-circle with identical computers, printers, and scanners at each seat. Steven sat at his father's workstation.

He began reading their notes:

Ben Nevis is the highest mountain in the British Isles. It is located at the western end of the Grampian Mountains close to the town of Fort Williams. Stranding 1,345 meters above sea level, the face of the north side is shear granite.

Steven put down the book. "I would be willing to bet that the face of that mountain is riddled with caves. Wow! This is more interesting than I thought." Steven spent most of the afternoon reading the notes and exploring the photo CDs of his parents' journey. The pictures made Ben Nevis come alive in a way that the notes hadn't. He was buried so deep in the books that he didn't hear Aunt Celia call him for dinner.

Bastet jumping at the word, 'dinner', startled Steven. He reluctantly closed the books, replaced them on the shelf and ran upstairs.

"You're spending too much time in the basement," Aunt Celia said.

After dinner, he tried to watch a rerun of the *Simpson's* and a movie, mostly to please his aunt. She was curled up on the couch reading a thesis from one of her Computer Science graduate students. Steven was a little in awe of her accomplishments, with her PhD and, until recently, serving as Chair of the Computer Science Department at Harvard. He wished he could tell her his secret, but The Seeker had made it clear that sharing his secrets could endanger her and jeopardize their mission. Still…

Aunt Celia wondered what was making Steven so antsy. "Steven, is there something you want to tell me? I'm a good listener."

Steven wished he could, but Bastet was eying him as if she knew what he was about to do. "No, Aunt Celia. I'm fine. Just all that pizza and soda yesterday."

Aunt Celia sighed. Someday, he'll trust me, she thought.

Steven tried to focus on the movie, but every so often, caught his aunt studying him. After it was over, Steven yawned and got up from the couch. He was about to go up to his room, but his hand found Aunt

Celia's card in his pocket. He went over and kissed his aunt good night on the cheek. "Thanks for helping me clean up. Thanks for everything."

"You're welcome, Steven! Have a good night's sleep, dear."

Steven headed for his room, wondering how Bastet always seemed to know ahead of time where he was going. His aunt had wished him a good night's sleep. He peered up the stairs and hoped that a good night's sleep was all that was waiting for him behind his door.

Chapter 9

Steven did not know what snapped him awake.

He lay very still, his heart racing and the sheet pulled up tight around his neck. He saw nothing unusual in the darkened room. *My imagination is running amok!* He was about to turn on the table lamp when he heard muffled sounds at the foot of his bed. Where had he heard those sounds before?

There it was again!

His mind raced to identify the sounds, but without success.

A strong smell hit his nostrils. *And what about that smell?* Steven, at first did not recognize the smell, but it seemed familiar…But what was it?

Steven turned his head in the direction of the sounds but saw only blackness. And then a pair of bright red eyes appeared to be floating toward him.

Steven gasped. "It's the Dark Ruler!" He was about to leap from his blanket when he heard a low growling sound.

Escape! He had to get out of the bedroom! Get down to his parent's lab! He could escape through the Portal! He couldn't move. Fear had him pinned down.

The eyes were a few feet away.

Steven saw the foam on the monster's lips. He had to do it! "Now!" Steven twisted right, threw back the covers, and leaped to the floor, running toward the door.

Bastet, who had been sleeping on Steven's bed, jumped onto the floor and raced after him.

Steven took the stairs two steps at a time and ran through the cellar hallway, finally reaching the lab. He punched in the lock code. Nothing! He did it again. The lock would still not open.

"Why?" he yelled, taking a deep breath, trying to keep his shaking hand still, as he re-entered the numbers.

The bolt popped open.

Was it too late?

Steven pushed the door open. He expected the demon to leap at him before he could set foot into the lab, but there was no sound of anything charging behind him. He turned, expecting to see the red eyes of the Dark Ruler, but the hallway was empty. "Strange!" he thought. "He's not following me."

He heard muffled footsteps on the ceiling above the corridor. "Oh, no! Not Aunt Celia!" He screamed out her name again and again, praying she heard him, praying she escaped.

"Steven are you ever getting up today?"

"That's Aunt Celia's voice," Steven mumbled to Bastet who had watched helplessly as Steven had been fighting invisible demons in his sleep. He blinked his eyes and searched his room. "Darn, Bastet, that was some nightmare!"

Bastet wondered if the boy was alright. Perhaps all this pressure was too much for any mortal, even the boy of the prophecy.

Steven glanced in the mirror. "I look like I've been in a war," he said to the cat.

Bastet was too busy preening herself to pay attention.

"Steven, are you coming down for breakfast?" Aunt Celia called up the stairs.

"I'll be down in a few minutes," he replied, hoping his aunt hadn't heard him screaming. The last thing he wanted was to have to explain to her what was really causing his nightmares.

Chapter 10

It was 10:30 am by the time Steven entered the lab. The Seeker was waiting for him.

"Good morning," Steven mumbled.

"You don't look rested, Steven."

"I had a bad dream." *That's an understatement! Believing the Ruler had invaded my room last night gave me nightmares.* He booted up his father's computer and soon found the location of Glen Coe.

"Where do you want the Portal arrival point? It needs to be someplace where I won't hit any walls or obstacles at the other end."

"I understand. Not being immortal, that is an important consideration. I guess our first arrival should be below the north wall."

"First? How many 'trips' do you think we'll need to make?" Steven asked, dreading the answer.

"I don't know—the fewer the better, of course. We don't want the Guardian to find out and alert the Ruler of Darkness what we're up to."

"Right! But the north side is 1,345 meters straight up," said Steven, looking at the mountain on his screen. "How can we possibly find the Guardian?"

The Seeker frowned. "We won't! He'll find us."

Steven didn't like the way he said that. "What do you mean?"

"This quest is a little different than our last."

"They're all a little different," Steven said, wishing The Seeker would stop beating around the bush.

The Seeker shrugged his thin shoulders. "Do you remember I told you yesterday that there have been several violent deaths over the past year from climbers falling. All unexplained."

"Yes. I remember that." Steven felt goosebumps rising on his flesh.

The Seeker's voice lowered. "Campbell is already awake."

"What? Who's awake?" Steven felt as if The Seeker had just punched his panic button. "What are you talking about?"

"Campbell."

"Why?"

"Let me finish?" The Seeker wished he could put his hands-on Steven's shoulders to calm him but knew he didn't have that power. "You must learn patience, Steven."

When a murder is involved, I can't be patient, Steven thought, wishing The Seeker would get to the point.

"You have seen the face of the wall? There are a number of caves several hundred meters high leading into the mountain. The largest entrance is just above the bottom of the cliff. It is a massive complex with tunnels leading deep into the mountain."

"And the Guardian. Where is he located?"

"The Ruler of Darkness sealed Campbell deep within the center of the mountain," The Seeker said. "He was to wait until he would be needed in the final battle against the MacDonalds."

Steven shivered. He knew now that the Dark Ruler had concealed his Guardians, mindless slaves, in an unknown number of tombs in every corner of the world. They were his secret army just waiting for his command to annihilate humanity. "So, what happened?" he asked.

The Seeker searched his memory. "While the cavers struggled to explore the cave system, they found Campbells wooden coffin and broke it open. Fortunately, no caver has unearthed Campbell's soldiers. But by releasing him, there have been a number of deaths over the past three years."

"Looks like just another walk in the park," Steven said with a bitter smile on his face.

"Lovely, I know just the park in New Zealand," answered The Seeker.

"Forget it," Steven said.

The Seeker shrugged, not understanding why Steven would reject a wonderful day in the park.

* * *

The lab was quiet—the only sound was the cooling fan in the computer.

Steven saw The Seeker was studying him, but why was the cat staring at him too?

The Seeker knew Steven needed time to think. He wouldn't burden the boy with the one last piece of bad news ... not yet.

"Let me see if I've got this straight," Steven said, counting each point on his fingers. "We are going to travel in the Portal—tricky in itself—to Glen Coe, to release Captain Campbell's soul. And to top-it-off, is guarded by, how many English troops?

"I counted 15, plus or minus one," responded The Seeker. He dropped his hand.

"Somehow, I don't think the odds of surviving are in my favor."

"Correct. The odds, as you say, are not good. But you are not the only one who will die if we are not successful. As before, we have no choice; the prophecy is clear."

"Terrific! I won't care if I'm dead, will I?" He let out a deep sigh. "I guess someone has to do it. It might as well be me."

"That's the spirit! I will meet you here tomorrow night. Try to get some sleep. You look tired!"

"Did he have to use the word 'spirit'?" Steven grumbled as he watched The Seeker leave.

Chapter 11

Deep in his underground domain, the Ruler of Darkness slouched over his throne.

The light from the lava pits cast an eerie glow, as twisting columns of steam rose from the depths. Dozens of cone-shaped stalactites hung from the ceiling and stalagmites rose from the floor. The temperature was unbearable.

To the left and right of the Ruler's throne, two large, flesh-eating gargoyles dozed. Their black fur was matted with sweat from the intense heat, their stench overpowering.

The Ruler did not notice, and he wouldn't have cared anyway. He was blinded to all else by his fixation on one goal: "I want that boy! I must take revenge on my enemies for freeing my Guardian! Taking that puny mortal's soul will not be enough. No, I must break him first. I will make him bend to my will. But how?" He stared hard at the fiery pit. Finally, he burst into cruel laughter. "Yes! That will be the perfect punishment. I will make him suffer, suffer, suffer!" He slammed his fist on the chair.

The gargoyles sprang to their feet, growling and pulling against their chains, fearing another of his temper tantrums.

"Easy my pets! Your time will come, after I finish with him." He smiled at the vision. "I will cover the mortal with mud and hang him in a steel cage over the lava pit. The steam will do my work for me. I will sit back and enjoy watching that little fool suffering. Oh, the joy of hearing him scream in agony for such a delightfully long time." He dropped his hand on the gargoyle's head.

The beast didn't dare pull away, but fear was etched on its face. Even this rock-brained creature knew how quickly the master's temper could flare.

The Ruler petted the gargoyle absent-mindedly. He remembered his pleasure watching African pygmies baking other humans in just such a way. The victims struggled against their bindings as the fire started to dry the mud. "The heat must have been unbearable." He laughed. He remembered how his excitement grew as the humans cheered, bloodthirsty, while their victims cried pitifully for mercy. The pounding drums, smell of cooking flesh, the chanting, only increased his joy. "Oh, Yes! I love watching humans torture each other! But seeing that boy melt hanging over a pit will make my revenge extra-sweet." He closed his eyes in rapture. "And when he is almost well-done, I will steal his wretched soul and feed the cooked flesh to my pets! Raw or cooked, it makes little difference to you, eh, my dear servants?"

The gargoyles didn't understand what he was talking about, but they were grateful that for once the Master seemed calm.

Lost in his vicious day-dream, the Ruler did not see Batena fly into the chamber. She was after all, no longer than a man's thumb.

Soaring down to the stone floor, Batena let out a high-pitched squeal. The gargoyles jumped to attention.

"Batena!" The Ruler shouted, "I have been waiting for your report. What news is there from Drooling Slayer? I'm sure you've found the boy and The Seeker?" He peered around the room. "Where are they?"

"Not yet found," Batena squealed, but—"

"You have not found the boy?" The Ruler leaned forward, temper simmering. "It has been two weeks since I sent you to Egypt. With every passing day, the trail grows cold. You must not fail in finding them, do you hear me?" He aimed his eyes at the bat.

"Yes," squeaked Batena, now much more nervous. "Problem, your Evilness—"

"What problem?"

"Night search only."

"Night search only?" He smiled broadly. "I see what you mean. I had not considered that you are a nocturnal predator..."

Batena giggled. "Yes. I night creature."

The Ruler nodded his head. "And I suppose Drooling Slayer, and the dragon, have difficulty seeing in the dark as well?"

Batena nodded her head happily, relieved the Master understood her problem.

The Dark Ruler tapped his fingers lightly on the armrest. "Yes, I can see the search would be much more difficult and take longer—" He appeared to be considering this problem when suddenly he screamed, "Are you kidding me? You dare to use an excuse such as this? I will provide you eyes to search for this boy." He leaped from his throne.

The gargoyles cowered closer to the throne.

"Look up at me, you lowly bat!" The Ruler commanded. His eyes turned blood red, flames appearing in their center. "I said, look upon your Master!"

The bat wanted to look away, but the Dark Ruler's eyes held her like magnets.

The Ruler was quaking violently and then shot a dark reddish beam at the bat from his burning eyes.

The bat let out a horrified scream, "I'm blind! I'm blind!"

The gargoyles shivered, wishing they could run away.

The Dark Ruler let out an evil laugh.

The bat was on the floor writhing in terror and pain.

"Don't be so dramatic," The Ruler said. "Open your eyes. You're not blind."

The bat opened her eyes. She wished she kept them closed since now she could see the Ruler glaring down at her.

"Can you see me now?" The Dark Ruler asked, barely holding back his fury.

The bat scrambled to her feet. "Yes. Yes. It's a miracle. You did it, my all-powerful Master who I will serve faithfully, loyally, always and always and—"

The Ruler grabbed the terrified bat in his fist and spoke each word as if it was a dagger plunging into Batena's tiny heart, "You now have eyes that see in the darkest dark. You will return to that fool, Drooling Slayer, and continue the search for that blasted boy and The Seeker." He held the bat close to his eyes. "Do not return until you have found them. Do you understand?" He tossed the bat to the floor.

'Oh, yes Master. Yes, Master. Batena understand." Batena leaped from the floor and shot directly for the venting tube leading out of the Ruler's lair.

The Ruler returned to his throne. "I enjoyed that." He dropped his hand on the gargoyle. "Boy, when I find you, I will inflict the most excruciating pain on your miserable body and then own your soul forever!" He closed his eyes, hoping that lovely vision of the boy hanging over the pit would reappear and calm his jangled nerves.

Chapter 12

Steven walked up the winding brick driveway toward Scotty's house. "This has to work," he mumbled as he reached the front door. Pressing the doorbell, he waited. When the door opened, he smiled at Mrs. Davis.

"Come, in Steven. Scotty is upstairs in his room waiting for you. How is your aunt?"

"Very well and busy as usual," replied Steven.

"Go on up. I'll call you when lunch is ready."

"Thanks, Mrs. Davis." Steven hurried up the stairs and knocked on the door decorated with signs suggesting the person entering this room use caution. After a pause, he knocked harder.

"Come in," Scotty replied.

Steven always laughed entering Scotty's room. He recalled the first time he was invited up to 'the den', as Scotty called it. That had been a year ago, after they first met at the Portsmouth Abbey. The yellow sign hanging on the door—showing men digging a hole—said it all.

Steven turned the doorknob and stepped in. The sun light in the hallway cast a long shadow into the cluttered room before he shut the door. He waited for his eyes to adjust before picking his way between stacks of clothes on the floor. Nothing had changed since his last visit. Cardboard boxes, cables, and card tables were crammed between the walls and bed. Every table was strewn with hard drives, gutted desktops, wires, computer chips, PC boards in various stages of dismemberment, and various power supplies. The air conditioner hummed in the corner next to the window.

When Steven first saw his friend's bedroom, Scotty told him that his parents had given up in trying to get him to clean it. He was free to do with it as he pleased, as long as he did not burn down the house or leave food around. His mother wisely never entered his room, having given up on getting it tidied. He put his dirty clothes and sheets on the chair outside his door, and she left the clean stuff on the same chair. It was like staying out of a lion's den, much safer that way.

"Sit anywhere," Scotty said, as Steven walked over to the desk unsure of where to sit.

Scotty sat back in his leather swivel chair, eyes glued to the center screen as his fingers pressed against the controls.

Steven watched in amazement as Scotty, in a matter of seconds, managed to slay three dragons, four gargoyles, blow up a door, and fire ten arrows at armored men racing away from an unknown pursuer. The noise emitted from the two large speakers as he destroyed the opponents was deafening. Then a banner flashed across the screen proclaiming Scotty the winner and displaying '75,000 points' and an invitation to proceed to the fourth level. "You're getting good at that," Steven said, impressed with Scotty's score.

"It's taken me an hour to master this level," Scotty announced with a broad smile. "So, what's the problem?" Scotty turned off the game.

Steven dumped some books and papers from a chair and sat down. "I'd like to be able to access computer files from my father's computer through my smart phone—"

"Now, why would you want to do that?" Scotty rocked back and forth in the chair.

"I want to be able to read my parent's computer files when I'm at school and on field trips, such as our upcoming trip to Scotland."

"What you want is to access their hard drives and the files they contain as if you were sitting in front of your home screen?" Scotty stopped rocking and leaned forward in the chair. "I have never tried this before, but I see no reason why it can't be done. Do you have your phone with you?"

Steven reached into his jacket pocket and handed it over.

Scotty took the phone and turned it over in his hand. "This won't be easy. Why didn't you ask your aunt to do this for you?"

Steven didn't want to reveal more than he had to. "I don't think Aunt Celia would agree to let me modifying the phone."

"Fair enough." Scotty rolled the chair in front of the first screen.

Steven watched Scotty maneuver the mouse and start tapping in key strokes to unlock the screen.

Scotty removed the rubber cap from the external port on the bottom of the phone and plugged in a long gray cable attached to the tower located beneath his desk. Next, he slipped on his earphones from his music pod and started rocking his head and shoulders to the music.

"This will take a while," Scotty said over his shoulder. "Got to get past the security walls and tap into the software to modify the program. First, we need the password used by the developer …."

Steven nodded. He knew better than to try to follow what Scotty was doing.

"Eureka!"

Steven jumped. "What happened?"

"Tell me I'm not good! In fact, I'm a genius!" Scotty laughed. Steven moved around Scotty to look at the screen.

"This is the code developed by the programmers that controls access to the web. What I need to do is modify the software and add a few sub-routines here which will allow you to access your computer's hard-drive when you dial home."

"Sub-routines?"

"Never mind." Scotty laughed, as he turned to face the monitor, and started tapping the keyboard again.

Steven was deep in thought. It would be handy to have someone like Scotty on the team. He was tempted to let him in on the secret of the prophecy and all he'd been through but knew it could place his friend in terrible danger. Could he really do that to a good friend?

Chapter 13

Steven used most of the morning preparing for his first trip to Glen Coe. Still not fully aware of how to program the Portal, a sort of time machine, he set the timer on the computer to open the Portal every fifteen minutes. Although this was not the ideal solution, it would have to do until he could figure out how to input the proper time for it return to pick him up from where he might be with his modified phone. The biggest problem: He hoped that nothing human, or non-human, would go through when it opened. Imagine if a creature like the Devourer accidentally stepped into the portal! Unfortunately, without knowing how to control it, he had no choice.

Bastet mewed, as if she read his mind.

Steven shook his head. "I wish I understood that cat." He pulled out his leather backpack from the cabinet. It had proven invaluable during the Egyptian trip. Steven had placed special equipment in the many pockets for speedy access. Top on his list were the red phosphorous flares. They had saved his life. He removed the last four flares from the box. "Not good! We'd better take more." He looked around the basement lab, when he stumbled across a large box containing a flare gun and a dozen cartridges. He threw the gun and four red cartridges in his pack. "I hope that's all I'll need!" he mumbled.

When he finally hit the pillow, he was exhausted, but couldn't get to sleep. He knew The Seeker would be in the lab in only a couple of hours. How could anyone sleep knowing what that meant?

* * * * * *

The alarm was ringing.

Steven lay still, listening to the sounds of the old house before reaching under his pillow and turning off the alarm. He had always felt safe in this house, even with the strange decor of the rooms, filled with relics and souvenirs his parents had brought home from their many trips to exotic countries.

Steven remembered the first time he'd seen the house. He was 12 and frightened of everything strange. It was on a cold, gray, December day, just before Christmas. Deep snow blanketed the grounds. The gray and brown stone-fronted house sat at the end of a long curving driveway almost hidden from Indian Avenue. Massive trees draped over the roof. They looked like giant creatures whose arms appeared to be reaching toward the windows of the house. To make it even more forbidding, the house overlooked the Sakonnet River, a black presence in the moonless night. And, as if all that wasn't enough, a statue of a Griffin sat on a stone ledge above the entrance to the house, with two Gargoyles guarding the yard from the roof's high corners. Creepy. He'd wondered if the house was haunted.

Steven laughed. Being haunted by ghosts would have been an improvement over having to deal with the prophecy. "You were right, Mom," Steven said to the empty room, "No ghosts, but Mom, I wish I could see you and Dad again."

Bastet let out a sad meow.

Yawning, Steven got out of bed, grabbed his clothes, and hurried to the bathroom.

Bastet let out an impatient meow.

"Let's go, Bastet," Steven said, when he'd dressed.

The house was eerily silent as Steven headed to the basement. The last thing he wanted was to wake up Aunt Celia. "She'll never understand," he said to Bastet who was running ahead. *I don't understand.*

As soon as Steven entered the lab, The Seeker appeared in a puff of smoke.

I wish he would show me how to do that trick, Steven thought.

"Are you prepared for our next journey, my young friend?" The Seeker asked, wishing he did not have to expose Steven to such danger.

"I've got my gear packed." Steven showed off his backpack.

"That's fine. Were you able to place the Portal's arrival point at the entrance of the cave? That is critical. We don't want you crashing into the granite wall."

"Yes, I think so. I also programmed the Portal to open every fifteen minutes after we arrive. When I get back, I'll work on a program to dial-up the Portal from my phone. I don't want to have some creature enter our house through the Portal." He could almost see Aunt Celia's terrified face.

"That would be terrible." The Seeker saw Bastet was pawing the ground impatiently. "I see one of us is ready to go."

Bastet mewed and showed her claws.

Steven grabbed his battery unit and put on his helmet. "I'm ready now if you are," Steven announced, trying to sound braver than he felt.

"Awesome! I believe that is the word you mortals use for such situations."

Steven laughed. "There's hope for you yet, Seeker."

Walking over to the computer, Steven moved the arrow on the screen over to the Portal icon on the upper left of the monitor, and double clicked the left button on his mouse.

Within seconds, the Portal appeared.

"I'm amazed when it does that," Steven said, quickly locking up the screen to make sure no one could change the settings. If that happened, he would be lost forever in some strange location.

This is your last chance to back out, Steven told himself. He could feel the change in temperature as he moved closer to the shimmering orb. He glanced at The Seeker, looked down at Bastet, and stepped through what looked like a kaleidoscope of liquid light.

Instantly he was surrounded by what appeared to be a million tiny stars. He lost all sense of direction. Was he floating, falling, or being sucked through a black hole in outer space? The small lights he had seen before were now a swirling blur. He felt cold, then hot. Was he wet or dry? He couldn't tell. He also couldn't tell how long it was before the Portal thumped lightly on landing.

Stepping through, he found himself back safe in the lab. "It works," he said.

"You have done well, boy of the Prophecy. Soon, we must use this device to find our next Guardian."

"But after I return from our trip to Scotland," Steven said, hoping The Seeker had remembered.

A dark look appeared on The Seeker's face. "There is something you should know about Scotland," he said.

"Another secret?" Steven asked, thinking no country in the world was completely safe for him now that he knew the prophecy.

Chapter 14

The next three weeks passed quickly. Steven completed his summer project and prepared for the much-looked-forward-to class trip to Scotland. But, at the same time, fearing that any day he might be needing it again, he kept testing the Portal.

Steven wasn't sure it would work and knew if it failed, he could be stranded in some far-off dangerous place without hope of ever getting back. He ran test after test to ensure the system was working correctly. He selected three different locations on the south end of Aquidneck Island. Over three nights, Steven and Bastet transported to those 'close' locations and returned. The software worked flawlessly. But would it work for longer trips? There was no way to test that without taking huge risks.

Steven's excitement grew as the day approached to fly to Scotland. His aunt had gone over their travel itinerary, nervously verifying they had their Passports, money, warm clothing, and loading him with travel brochures. "You don't have to be so nervous," he said, wondering how he was going to carry everything. "You're going with me as a chaperone. Remember?" He almost wished she wasn't and hoped she wouldn't hover over him like this in front of all his friends.

Aunt Celia nodded, but went over all his supplies again.

Steven couldn't wait to close his suitcase and get this trip going.

Arriving at Logan Airport at 5:00 p.m., the busload of kids and their chaperones disembarked and were herded into small groups. Aunt Celia had volunteered to watch Paul, Scotty, Rusty, Charlie, and of course Steven.

"We need a name for our group," Aunt Celia announced full of cheer. "I know. We'll call ourselves 'The Scotland Rockers!" She gave a happy laugh.

"Oh, no," Rusty muttered.

It could be worse, Steven thought as he picked up his suitcase. The Scotland Rockers were on the move.

"Scotland here we come," Paul shouted. "I can't wait."

"How many rooms do you think they will let us into when we tour Edinburgh and Stirling Castles?" Charlie asked, looking up from a brochure about the castles.

"Boys, let's get checked in and head for our gate," Aunt Celia said, looking like a mother hen as she nudged the group toward the ticket counter. "Isn't this going to be fun?" She asked, giving Steven a little poke.

Steven wondered.

****

They arrived in Edinburgh the next morning, tired but excited to be through customs and heading for their hotel. After Aunt Celia checked them in, the boys headed to their rooms where they nearly collapsed on their beds.

"Gather around, boys," Aunt Celia said when they met for lunch. "We won't meet our tour guide and get our schedule for visiting Glasgow and the surrounding countryside until tomorrow. Therefore, we're on our own for the rest of the day. What do you say to exploring the city?"

With all in agreement, Aunt Celia led the charge up to the Royal Mile. The shops and quaint streets fascinated them, and the afternoon passed quickly. The smell of food drove them to a small restaurant for dinner where they were treated to an assortment of Scottish food at a buffet. The tables were loaded with such dishes as steak pie, roast chicken, fish, mince and potatoes, baked ham, peas, roasted potatoes, Cockaleekie Soup (Chicken and Leeks), pork pie, and meat pie. All left the table stuffed and hardly able to move let alone make their way back to the hotel. Even Steven was beginning to relax, forgetting that at any second something might interrupt this wonderful vacation.

The following morning after a hardy Scottish breakfast: fried eggs, porridge, bacon, toast, and broiled tomatoes the groups gathered at the bus station where they boarded busses that took them to the train station and a day-trip to Glasgow.

For the next three days, they rode the Scottish Rail and busses around the countryside. They visited Inverness to view Loch Ness on the second day. Steven was disappointed that Nessie was nowhere to be seen, but thought perhaps after all he'd been through, that wasn't such a bad thing.

They toured Stirling Castle on the third day, and Edinburgh Castle on day four.

"Not one ghost," Rusty complained.

Thank goodness, Steven thought, quite content to leave ghosts at home.

On the final day, prior to leaving for home, they all walked along the Royal Mile and a tour of Edinburgh's legendary Underground City was scheduled. The students were again divided between the three red and blue busses waiting for them outside the hotel.

Bus 1, loaded with Mr. Brown's group, to start their tour at Greyfriars Cemetery to see the statue of Greyfriars Bobby, the Skye terrier, who according to the guidebook, remained at his master's gravesite for fourteen years, until his death in 1872. Steven wondered if Bastet would do that for him if the Dark Ruler defeated him. He knew the cat would do whatever it took to protect him, but wondered if it was out of affection, or just duty to the prophecy.

Steven's was happy his group was heading to Mary King's Close. He knew there were many stories about ghosts walking the old vaults, roaming the hidden caverns and streets of the Underground City. He listened as his friends excitedly shared their little ghost stories while the bus headed for the Royal Mile.

"I can't wait to see a ghost," Paul said. "I heard you can feel the temperature get icy cold in the stone rooms." He smiled knowingly, "That means you might feel the touch of a ghost, or even see one."

Steven smiled thinking they had no idea what they could run into. He knew too well.

Arriving at the entrance to Mary King's Close, the boys stood waiting impatiently to file into the shop to purchase their tickets. Within minutes, they were ushered down wooden steps into a small dark room. They waited for the tour guide to speak.

The guide, giving them a sinister smile, warned them of the closeness of the walls they would pass through. "Ye might even be seeing little Annie, the young girl searching endlessly for her parents."

An eerie silence enveloped the group as the guide finished his introduction.

"What do you think? Will we see a ghost?" Scotty asked Steven as they waited at the end of the short line.

"From what I read in the book you gave me, we have a good chance of seeing one," Steven replied, not really swallowing the tour guide's stories.

They started down the narrow alleyway.

"Can you feel the change in temperature?" Scotty murmured.

Steven, known as the scientific type, replied that the temperature was normally 55° Fahrenheit and not the result of any ghost waiting to waylay them.

Scotty wasn't convinced.

Steven realized he'd been right not to include him on The Seeker's team.

As they walked down the long dimly lit passageway, Steven could just barely make out a doorway to the left of the tour guide.

As the group passed the door, Steven stepped inside. What was he sensing? Switching on his flashlight Steven peered at the crude stone walls and dirt floor. His light revealed two mannequins, one dressed as a woman, and the second, as a man in dirty, tattered clothes. They were sitting across from each other at a table. He looked closer and saw they were hunched over the wooden table resting on their elbows, each holding a wooden spoon, a bowl of what appeared to be gruel in front of them. A loaf of bread lay to the left of the man's elbow and a slice of cheese was clenched in the woman's hand.

A hand landing on his shoulder made Steven jump.

Chapter 15

The guide lifted his hand off Steven's shoulder. He gave Steven that sinister grin. "Ye best not lose us, lad, or ye could be stuck in the sixteen-hundreds with our friends here."

"Come on Steven," Scotty called. "The guys are almost out of sight."

"I'll be there in a minute," Steven called, as he entered another room. He aimed his flashlight around the room. It was cold, colder than he expected. His flashlight shot up as a shadow appeared to flicker on the opposite wall. He stared at the spot where he thought he'd seen something move. "It must have been my imagination," he muttered, "Not strange considering everything." He aimed the flashlight again, but this time there was no movement.

Steven, not realizing the group was no longer near, remained a moment longer, flashlight circling the room, before stepping out onto the street. He was alone.

Steven tried to listen for the voices of his friends. Unable to hear anything, Steven decided to try to find them by walking down the left side of the street. He inspected each doorway and alleyway, hoping they would be there.

It was quiet without them. He was beginning to enjoy being alone for a change. As long as there was light, he was fine.

As if on cue his flashlight went out.

What?! Not now, franticly switching the light on and off. Nothing. He banged the flashlight against the palm of his hand. No luck.

"Great," he muttered, stuffing the flashlight into his pant leg pocket. "It really is dark here." He continued to search the dimly lighted rooms along the alleyway. "If this happened before I met The Seeker," he thought, "this darkness would have really scared me. What a difference a few months make!"

When Steven was nervous, he sometimes talked to himself, and not finding his friends was making him very nervous. "Of course, it only took a search in a tomb, a battle against the Devourer, and the help of The Seeker to overcome my fear of darkness." Steven shivered as a bone chilling sensation ran up his spine. "I'm not afraid of anything anymore. Where did Scotty and the others get off to?"

Suddenly, Steven shivered again. The temperature had dropped, and he noticed vapor from his breath rising in front of him. What was happening? Could it really be a ghost?

He moved inside a doorway and pressed against the door. He felt strange, colder. He tightened his hands into fists, eyes locked on the storefront directly across the street. "I'm safe as long as I hide here until the others come back to look for me," he convinced himself.

Steven did not see a figure materialize behind him, in the vacant room.

An ice-cold hand slipped into his.

Looking down, he saw a small child in a long, tattered dress staring up into his eyes. He wanted to pull his hand away but didn't dare. He didn't dare move.

When the girl didn't move either, Steven turned to see her again. Her hair was matted, wet-looking and her face appeared to be scarred, scratch marks on both cheeks. "Who are you?" he asked.

The girl did not say a word as she pulled Steven away from the doorway, down a small alleyway.

Steven wondered if he could fight her off, break free, but couldn't seem to break away.

She led him to a door, which opened soundlessly.

Steven, still held by that small icy hand, looked around the walls of the empty room, wondering why he had been brought here.

As if in answer, the gray stones started to vibrate and fall to the stone floor. When the last stone rolled to a stop, the child pulled Steven's hand again, leading him through the hole.

Hearing a noise behind him, Steven stopped. He turned back, thinking he could escape, but saw the rocks mysteriously were fitted back into the wall. The entrance was sealed. I'm trapped, he thought, wishing the girl's hand would let him free. "Where are you taking me?" Steven asked, as his panic meter began to rise.

"Follow the girl, Steven." A low raspy voice came from a blurred face gradually appearing in front of him.

"Who are you?" Steven tried to pull away from the little girl's hand.

"Names are meaningless here." The face was now fully formed, revealing multiple oozing sores.

Steven shivered at the horrifying sight, but the hand still held him. "I want to go home," he said.

"I have been asked to lead you to our gathering place," the ghostly voice said.

"Who asked you?" Steven demanded, wishing he could reach into his pack and find something that would free him.

"The Seeker."

"The Seeker is here?" Steven shook off the fear that had been racing through his body. "For real? The Seeker sent you?"

Steven felt more relaxed as the girl pulled him along in the dark. As they advanced, he thought he heard someone calling his name. It sounded as if it was from behind the wall. There was a faint light up ahead and the girl was walking faster.

"Slow down! I can't keep up!"

Suddenly, Steven found himself staring at a large open street filled with men, woman, and children in tattered clothing hurrying in and out of alleyways, rushing in and out of dilapidated buildings. "Are all these people real?" he asked, feeling tense again in this strange place with all these ghostly figures.

"These are my friends," the girl said, still not letting go of Steven's hand.

"What is this place? Who are all these people?"

The girl gazed sadly into his eyes. "This is a hidden part of the city no one ever sees. The people around us are those souls seeking loved ones long entombed in these buildings during the great plague."

Entombed? Not again, Steven thought.

"Yes, Steven, as the plague ran rampant, many families were forced to take refuge throughout the old city to prevent bands of police from finding them."

"Why would they hide from the police?"

The girl sighed. "Once the infected people were found, the police would gather them together."

"To help them?"

The girl laughed. "No. To place them in these terrible rooms. Once the rooms were full, they would seal the entranceway. They would let them die." The girl's eyes grew hard. "My parents are among the missing."

"I'm sorry," Steven said. "Why did you bring me here?"

"I asked Annie to bring you," said The Seeker.

Chapter 16

Steven turned around and saw The Seeker dropping gently to the ground. The girl was no longer holding his hand. He searched for her, but she had disappeared. "She sounded so sad. I wanted to help her."

The Seeker dropped his hand on Steven's shoulder. "I'm afraid we don't have much time. Your aunt has realized you are no longer with the group and is searching the old city. I need to talk to you and thought this would be the best place."

"Annie mentioned the plague. Is that what this is about?"

"Yes. The records show that of the 40,000 residents that lived in old Edinburgh only 60 survived when the Black Plague ended in 1645."

"Let me guess, the Ruler of Darkness had a hand in this?"

The Seeker nodded. "He was not totally responsible, but he did have a major hand in ensuring that it killed as many people as possible before it finally ended."

"What can we do about that?" Steven asked. "Even if I wanted to help, we're leaving—"

"Yes, I know." The Seeker smiled. "I need you to ask your aunt to extend your vacation, so you can take a side trip to Glen Coe in the highlands."

"Glen Coe?"

"Yes. There you will search for the dragon."

"Dragon?" Steven asked, a bewildered expression on his face. "Did you say dragon?"

"*Yes, dragon.*"

"Tell me I am not dreaming this?"

"Unfortunately, you're not dreaming."

Steven shook his head hard to be certain he wasn't dreaming this whole thing up. Finally, he asked, "But what reason do I give Aunt Celia? You know how she is."

"Yes. Stubborn, difficult, nosy, but very caring. I know. Tell your aunt that you want to see more of the country and that the highlands have always been an area you've wanted to see. Glen Coe runs right along the West Highway footpath, a mountain trail that stretches ninety-five miles between Glasgow and Fort William. You must convince her that this has been your dream forever. Now go! You have got to get back to your group." He waved his arm. "Annie, my little one, please lead Steven back to where you found him. I have preparations to make."

Steven watched The Seeker fly off into the darkness, as Annie's cold hand once again slid into his.

Annie led Steven past crowds of sad people milling around in the streets. "You must come back to help them someday," she said softly and disappeared in the mist by the shop where he had first seen her.

"I don't believe this!" Steven said.

"What don't you believe?" Scotty asked, hurrying toward Steven. "Where have you been? We've been looking for you all over."

"Steven are you alright?" Aunt Celia asked. "You look like you've seen a ghost?"

"I'm fine, Aunt Celia." Steven tried to smile, as he looked around to see where he was. "You won't believe this, but I was talking to Annie just before you called my name. She was standing right next to me holding my hand."

Aunt Celia shook her head. "You have some imagination, dear boy."

Steven shook himself back to the present. It was better if his aunt thought it was all in his imagination. He could imagine how she'd react if she thought the ghost was real.

When the group entered a room where Annie had lived, the tour guide told the boys there were many reports of a ghost child by others who claimed to have seen her. "Aye, Annie was seen on many occasions, always searching for her lost doll." He pointed to a corner of the room. "This accounts for the number of dolls stacked against the wall over here. They are all left by visitors for the poor little girl searching for her doll forever."

Steven knew Annie was searching for far more than her doll, but how could he correct the tour guide? Who would believe him that he had been touched by the ghost and led to the hidden part of the city where so many spirits were still searching for their family members who had been victims of the plague and the drastic measures the authorities took to stop it from spreading. He could almost feel that tiny icy hand in his again and shivered at the memory. I will come back, he promised as he followed the Rockers away from the shops.

The rest of the day passed quickly as the group moved from the Underground City, walked along the Royal Mile, toured the National Gallery, and ended up at the North Bridge. By the time they arrived back to the hotel it was 6:00 p.m. and time for supper. Everyone was abuzz with the excitement of the day, but Steven was oddly silent. He was thinking of The Seeker and what his friend had asked him to do.

Later that night Steven pulled his aunt aside. They were sitting in soft chairs in the hotel library, which was lined with book shelves and old-looking landscapes. Steven saw one that looked like it was of the highlands, grassy, but with storm clouds brewing overhead. "Aunt Celia, could we spend a few more days in Scotland?" he asked, anticipating her resistance.

Aunt Celia looked puzzled. "What do you have in mind?"

"I'd like to go to Glen Coe in the highlands. I've heard so much about it."

"Glen Coe?"

"Yes. I've heard it's beautiful. Like this painting." He pointed to the landscape on the wall. "I read that from Glen Coe you can see the Devil's Staircase."

Aunt Celia looked alarmed. "The Devil's Staircase? Now, why would you want to see that?"

Steven sensed he'd made a mistake. "Mom always said it was one of the most beautiful places she'd ever seen. She always promised that someday she would take me there."

Aunt Celia heard the longing in her nephew's voice. She knew he still missed his parents. If his mother had promised Steven that, how could she break that promise? "I think that's a wonderful idea," she replied, and then had another thought. "We could ask Rusty if he would like to join us. I understand he has nothing planned after we get back."

"Yes!" Steven's eyes lit up, but then he remembered the mission to search for the dragon. Would Rusty just get in the way?

"What a strange look on your face, Steven. Are you sure you're all right?"

Steven nodded, but wondered if he was placing his aunt and Rusty in unknown danger by including them in his mission.

Chapter 17

Mrs. Smith had consented to accompany Paul, Scotty, and Charlie on the return flight back to the States. After saying their good-byes at the Edinburgh Airport, Steven, Rusty, and Aunt Celia rented a silver four-door Vauxhall Astra and headed west on the A8 out of the city.

The weather during their trip from Edinburgh had been overcast, but the threat of rain never materialized. They traveled along the scenic route of A82 toward Glen Coe, then diverted from the main highway and headed to the Orchy Hotel and Inn for dinner. As they turned onto a long narrow street Steven saw rows of white-washed houses with thatched roofs dotting the surrounding landscape. The scene looked lovely and peaceful, so why didn't he feel that way?

The hotel and inn stood at the far end of the road. They parked the car and walked along the dirt road to the welcoming entryway. While waiting to be seated, the three looked at the pictures hanging on the wall leading into the dining area. They dated as far back as the 1800s and revealed that the inn and the surrounding homes were the original structures, mostly unchanged over hundreds of years.

While having dinner the group learned from their host that the hotel was built in 1708 and that the small road they had traveled on was one of the original roads constructed in 1751 into the highlands.

"Isn't that amazing?" Aunt Celia said, enjoying the history.

Rusty was too busy eating to reply, and Steven was thinking that the old buildings were the perfect setting for more ghosts.

Aunt Celia noticed Steven was very quiet, but thought it was because he was thinking of his parents. Sometimes it was better to just let him be.

The local fare, bagpipes hanging over the bar, and a fire ablaze in the wide mouth fireplace made for a pleasant dinner, but it was getting late. They checked into the Clachaig Inn, just outside the village of Glen Coe. Exhausted, they said their goodnights and went straight to bed.

Still dressed, shoes tossed to the floor, Steven lay on his back in the dark of the strange room. He tried to fall asleep but ended up listening to Rusty snoring in the next bed. He was glad his aunt agreed to this trip, but how was he supposed to free a dragon? What did The Seeker want him to do now? If the past was any clue, he knew he could be facing incredible danger.

Steven must have drifted off to sleep, because he was startled awake by a voice whispering in his ear. His eyes snapped open to find a dark, weathered face staring down into his eyes. He was about to scream, but clamped his mouth shut, his eyes landing on a long scar trailing down the face above him. "Who are you?" he asked, wishing Rusty would wake up and frighten this scary face from the room.

The spirit motioned Steven to get out of bed as he floated away from the bed to the center of the room.

Steven, still wary, rose and moved towards the spirit. He felt a chill as the apparition extended his hand luminescent in the darkness. He cautiously touched the rough hand and in the blink of an eye found himself outside, somewhere behind the hotel. "What?" He exclaimed, realizing he was standing barefoot on wet grass. "Where are we?" He saw several reddish cattle staring at him from over a fence. "How did you do that?"

"No time for chit-chat, laddie, I be Angus MacDonald, the laird of the clan." The ghost hissed with a deep Scottish brogue. "I be ordered to help ye' find the dragon held prisoner in the mountains of Glen Coe. Ye can't let Campbell get ahold of her or all havoc will break loose."

"I know that already, but where do I look? What do I do?" Steven wished someone would give him firm directions, so he could get this over with already.

"Patience, laddie," MacDonald said, "All in good time. First, ye goes north along the mountain trail jest outside of town until you get to the Devil's Staircase."

"I really have to go the Devil's Staircase?" Steven did not like the idea of going to a place with that name. "I really don't want to go there alone," he muttered.

The ghost smiled, revealing missing teeth. "Ye won'ts be alone. A flock of crows will identify where ye are to search." The ghost suddenly cocked his head as if he heard someone nearby, but then aimed his eyes at Steven. "Ye' best be on yer way now. We're all dependin' on ye."

"Wait a minute! Aren't you coming with me?" Steven wasn't sure if he wanted such a scary-looking companion, but also knew he didn't want to go to this Devil's place by himself.

The ghost sniffed the air. "No. I must return to my post to watch for reinforcements from Kinlochleven. The Guardian must not escape to the hills."

Steven had no idea what the ghost was talking about.

"It all rests on ye," he rasped and was gone.

Steven was standing next to his bed as if nothing had happened. Was it real or a dream? He suddenly realized his feet were cold and wet. He picked up his foot. There were grass clippings on the bottom. "Okay, it wasn't a dream." Steven wiped the grass off his feet, and then climbed back into bed. Thankfully, even though his mind was full of questions, he fell asleep.

Rusty woke around 7:30. "Hey Steven," he called, "Wake up. We got a great bike ride today."

Steven wished Rusty would let him sleep longer but heard the excitement in his friend's voice.

"I can't wait to get on that mountain bike ride. I hear the West Highway footpath is really a cool ride."

Steven smiled at his friend's eagerness. "The brochure I picked up yesterday from the Ballachulish Visitor Centre had a map of the entire trail and the towns along the way. It really does look cool."

"Last one ready is a rotten egg," Rusty shouted.

Steven jumped out of bed trying to get to the bathroom first but Rusty beat him to it and shut the door.

Sitting back down on the bed, Steven remembered MacDonald's visit last night. He wondered what he meant when he said he must return to his post? He visualized the soldier again and realized he was clad in a green, black, and blue plaid kilt that appeared tattered. He recalled thinking the blade of the sword hanging from his belt had been rusty and stained with red. That reminded him of Rusty's red hair. He was taking forever in the bathroom. "Will you please hurry?"

"Hold your horses!" Rusty shouted.

Steven sighed. The longer Rusty took, the more time he had to think. *I'm supposed to look for a dragon, a mythological creature? How? Where?* He glanced out the window. *A bunch of crows will show me. That's what he said.* Steven sighed again, realizing the one thing that was bothering him the most: *Why is The Seeker not here to help me?*

"Your turn," Rusty announced, finally leaving the bathroom. When Steven didn't answer, he said, "Steven, are you okay?"

"What?" Steven shook himself back to the present. "You're finally out! My turn in the bathroom at last." He raced into the room and slammed the door. Once he was alone again, he sagged against the wall. "Why isn't The Seeker here?" he asked his face in the foggy mirror. It occurred to him that with the mist on the mirror, he looked like a ghost.

Chapter 18

After the boys dressed, they went downstairs to the lounge. Aunt Celia was already there, reading the local newspaper.

"Morning, Aunt Celia," Rusty said cheerfully.

"Did you boys sleep well?" Aunt Celia asked, placing the paper on her lap. "Breakfast will be served shortly and after we eat, I thought we should head to town to take in the local scenery." She wondered why Steven was so quiet, but she decided again it was best to let him work it out himself. She knew he still didn't trust her enough to share everything with her. That would take time. She could wait.

After a large Scottish breakfast, eggs over easy, black pudding, fried tomatoes, sausage links, mushrooms, grilled kidneys, and potato scones, they piled into the car and headed for town.

Steven felt bloated from all the food he had eaten. "Aunt Celia, after all that food, I need exercise. Is it alright if Rusty and I rent mountain bikes and ride a few trails?"

Aunt Celia felt disappointed, but then quickly brightened up. "That's a great idea! While you two are doing that I will be shopping in the local stores."

Steven felt relieved. "Don't forget, we have to lug what you buy back home," he teased, grunting as if he were straining to pull a heavy suitcase.

Aunt Celia and Rusty laughed.

Only Steven knew why he wanted to ride into the mountains.

The day was clear. A light mist hung over the upper mountain ridges. Steven scanned up the mountains to see if he could spot crows. We're still too close to the Village, Steven thought. He turned his attention back to the cottages and other quaint buildings along the side of the road. He slipped his hand into his right pocket and pulled out the Amulet, placing it around his neck. *Never know what this day has in store for me. Without The Seeker and Bastet around, I'll need all the help I can get.*

After his aunt exited a roundabout, she parked across from a local chemist shop, which in the States is called a pharmacy.

Steven decided to sit on the bench outside while she and Rusty ventured inside.

Two locals sat on a bench, deep in a conversation.

"I am telling ye, I think a pack of dogs were responsible for the killing of McLean's sheep the other night," said a man wearing a dark green jacket.

"Nae," the other snorted. "McLean's son Andrew told me that there were no dog tracks anywhere near the carcass when he found it down by the berm. The sheep had been quartered with the shoulders and hind legs taken." He pulled on his pipe and then said. "He did see large footprints in the mud, along the water's edge."

Steven was curious now and noticed the men's faces were weathered; a light brown leathery color, their hands calloused probably from hard labor on farms.

The second man took the pipe from his mouth. "Andrew said he was going to search the hills."

"Tis most likely some vagrant up in the hills, feeding on the livestock and all."

"I would say so," agreed the other man as he puffed hard on his pipe and exhaled smoke between his sentences. "Ya think they would search the caves along the northern ridge where the British Troops hid, waiting to massacre the MacDonalds."

Steven sat back, a worrying thought in his brain. *I wonder if the butchering of the sheep has something to do with the dragon?*

"Steven." Rusty interrupted his thoughts. "There's a guy who owns a mountain bike shop half a mile down the road. Aunt Celia said she'll take us down there and lease the bikes we need for our ride up the trails."

"Great," Steven said, antsy to get going. "Let's get started."

Aunt Celia rented the bikes for two days. Steven and Rusty grabbed several bottles of spring water and some power bars for their adventure.

"Well, I guess we're ready," Rusty said.

I hope we are, Steven thought, still wondering if dragging Rusty along was a great idea.

"If you see men with guns don't be alarmed," the shop owner said.

"Guns?" Aunt Celia looked anxiously at Steven.

"Oh, nothin' to be alarmed about. They be local farmers searching for what's responsible for killing their sheep."

"Should I be worried?" Aunt Celia asked.

"No. Not at all. They be searching the north side of the mountain. Your boys will be riding the trails on the south side. Am I right, lads?"

Aunt Celia frowned. "I want you boys back before four o'clock."

"But Aunt Celia—" Steven began.

"No buts at all, Steven. Now, you both have a good time and be back on time or…well just be back." She thought of giving him a kiss on the cheek, but not in front of Rusty. Instead she added, "And if there is trouble, Steven, you use your phone and call me right away."

"Okay, Aunt Celia," Steven called over his shoulder eager to get away before she changed her mind. He started up the street toward the mountain trail.

The ride up the mountain was difficult with the steep incline. Both boys were breathing hard by the time they stopped at the top of the trail.

Steven looked north along the ridge of the mountain range and could see Ben Nevis, the highest rock formation in the Scottish Highlands. Long strips of what appeared to be ice lined the face of the mountain. Taking a second look, Steven realized these were individual waterfalls fed by the snowcaps atop the mountain ridge. He was searching for the crows.

"What are you looking for?" Rusty asked, gasping for air.

Steven still wasn't sure how much to tell Rusty. "According to the two old guys I talked to by the shop, there's a cavern here that was used by the British troops in 1692 to hide from the MacDonalds. They attacked while the clan slept. They wiped out almost the whole clan." "That happened in the villages of Glen Coe?" Rusty asked, now searching for the cave too.

Steven held his hand above his eyes to shield the sun's reflection off pools of water dotting the valley below. Windswept trees were scattered along the valley floor surrounded by dense brown grass and thick bunches of gorse. Red Highland cattle were grazing contentedly in the fields. The air was crisp with a slight breeze as Steven turned to look out over the west passage. Snow-capped mountains dotted the landscape in the distance. Still no crows.

"Let's keep moving," Rusty said. "I'm getting chilly."

"Okay," Steven said and pushed down hard on his right pedal. He was still not comfortable with Rusty getting involved in his search for the dragon, but he couldn't very well have told him not to come along! "There was no other way," Steven mumbled. His breathing was becoming heavier as the trail became steeper.

"Steven, did you hear that?" Rusty whispered as he pulled his bike parallel to where Steven was stopped gazing down the hill.

"Hear what?"

"I thought I heard a roaring sound coming from the rock formation above us."

Steven looked along the ridge above them. "The only thing I hear is the wind howling through the pines."

"I could have sworn that I heard a roar a moment ago. Maybe not." Rusty shrugged and started down the trail with Steven close behind.

As they rounded the bend, Steven saw a group of black birds sitting atop a large rock formation jutting out over the trail. They're here, he thought, astounded by the number of crows congregated in one spot.

The cawing sound was deafening as the boys approached.

"Can you believe this?" Rusty shouted over the noise.

"This is called a 'murder' of crows," Steven said, laughing.

"A what?" Rusty looked nervous.

"The proper name for a bunch of crows is a 'murder'. You know. Like 'herd of cattle' or 'flock of sheep.'"

"How do you know such weird stuff?" Rusty was backing away.

"I read!"

"I think we should go back," Rusty said, thinking such a large 'murder' of black crows was not a good sign.

Steven pulled a map from his backpack. "Our goal is Devil's Staircase, where it crosses the range six kilometers east of Meall Dearg."

"Devil's Staircase?" Rusty shivered. "I never said that was my goal."

Steven smiled. "I think we're midway between Kinlochleven and Glen Coe," he shouted over the din. "I think what we're looking for is up there, above the large boulder, where the crows are perched."

"How do you know?" Rusty looked up at the ravens, thinking maybe Steven was looking for it, but he wasn't, especially if it was something named after the devil.

Steven folded the map. "Let's push our bikes up to that large rock and hide them before we go on." As he pushed his bike up the rocky hill, he wondered how he was going to keep Rusty out of harm's way. *He mustn't become involved in the prophecy!* But how could he prevent it and still accomplish his mission?

Chapter 19

Drooling Slayer pressed himself hard against the cold gray boulder that overhung the trail below the mountain known as Ben Alder. The air was bitter cold, and a blanket of mist clung above him.

"At least no one will see me from here," he snorted.

He'd been shadowing a buck and three does walking along the mountain trail since dawn, hoping the buck would eventually lead the females to where he was waiting. Gripping his club tightly he waited. This was his second day of feasting on the wildlife in the Glen Coe mountains. Tomorrow he must feed the 'dragon' and then he'd continue searching for the boy.

The sound of pebbles being disturbed on the trail alerted him to the approaching deer. First approaching was a seven-point buck, followed a short distance behind by the does. Attacking the male could be dangerous. He waited for the last female.

The buck stopped and raised his head. His ears lifted, trying to pick out any sound that would alert him to danger. His nose twitched sniffing the air. Not picking up anything out of the ordinary, after shaking his huge antlers, threatening any unseen predator, the buck proceeded cautiously down the path.

Drooling Slayer remained perfectly still as each deer walked under the overhang.

When the last doe had just cleared the rock, he leaped from his hiding place onto her back.

A terrified scream burst from the doe's throat as Drooling Slayer's weight crashed down on her and her legs crumpled under her.

His club pounded hard on her skull and she lay still, tongue hanging from between her teeth, blood pooling around her mouth.

The Slayer, focused on the doe, drew back in alarm at the sound of the buck bellowing in rage.

The buck stepped in front of the two remaining females, snorted angrily, lowered his head, and pounded his hoof against the ground. He advanced toward Drooling Slayer and looked as if he was about to charge when suddenly he turned and ran after the females who he had protected so they could escape while he confronted the monster. Within seconds, the three deer disappeared into the mist.

Drooling Slayer roared in victory. With the buck no longer a threat, he placed the club in the sling around his belt and pulled his knife from its sheath. He thrust the blade into the deer's belly just under the ribcage and sliced toward her hind legs. Pulling back the skin, he reached for the liver. Blood ran down his arm. He continued tearing at the meat with brutal pleasure.

After satisfying his hunger, the Slayer ripped out the innards and tossed them on the ground. He wiped the blood from his knife and hands in the tall grass beside the trail. Grabbing the deer by the front and hind legs, he threw what was left of the carcass across his shoulders and started climbing up the gorge. He must find a place to hide and feast for the next several days.

Later that morning two villagers noticed crows circling low above the tree line. Knowing this was a sign of a recent kill, they hurried up the trail. They saw two black birds pulling the entrails apart.

When the birds saw the men, they dropped the meat and flew off cawing in protest at being disturbed.

The men drew closer.

"Well this confirms my suspicion as to who's been killing deer and sheep in the area," Sam, a ranger from the Wildlife authority, said, pointing at the strange footprints around the kill. "The killer had very wide, flat feet...like no animal I've ever seen." He got up from the ground and with his eyes followed the trail of footprints.

"I never seen no prints like these before either," Dick, a local hunter, muttered, looking hard at the prints as the trail headed up the mountain. He knew from experience that this weird, wild, and unearthly mountain, with its glacial moonscape and jagged rocks, would not easily yield the secret of where this unusual hunter had gone.

"He headed up toward the ridge over here," Sam said, climbing up the overhang. "This would be a good spot to jump a deer."

"The weather's getting cold," Dick said, still scanning the mountainous hills and valley below. "Whatever this thing is, I don't want to meet up with it in the dark."

Sam nodded. "Time to get back before the wind picks up and the rain starts. We'll resume our search tomorrow."

They both headed back down the hill toward the trail, listening for any warning that whatever had butchered the deer wasn't right behind them.

Chapter 20

"There it is again," shouted Rusty over the cawing of the crows huddled above. "It sounds like an animal is in pain." He quickened his pace over the loose stones.

Steven hurried up the slope, keeping well away from the pebbles, and shale pushed down by Rusty's boots.

"Over there," Rusty shouted. "There's a small opening in the mountain."

"I see it. We better hurry. I think it's starting to snow!"

"In August?" Rusty looked up.

"This is Scotland, remember?"

Both boys raced up the ridge and entered the tunnel. Sweat poured from their faces and their chests heaved from the rapid climb. They sat down on a flat bolder and waited to catch their breath.

Steven pulled the flashlight from his backpack and pressed the switch.

Rusty followed his lead.

Both scanned the walls.

Rusty saw the two tunnels leading into the mountain first. As usual, he wanted to lead. "We should split up, Steven. Why don't you take the tunnel on the right?"

Steven looked at his watch. He didn't like the idea of splitting up in the tunnels, but it could keep Rusty from learning the whole truth. "Okay, but let's meet back here in thirty minutes."

"Got it," Rusty said, and headed into the dark opening.

Steven hesitated. *I don't like this. What if he finds the dragon?* He aimed his flashlight and headed into the tunnel.

A short way down, he saw water dripping into a small pool to the left of the trail. As he walked deeper into the mountain, he felt the air thinning. Up ahead more water was trickling down the face of another flat gray rock wall. Suddenly, Steven thought he heard flapping noises up ahead. He stopped to listen, but all was quiet. The only sound he heard were his boots scuffing along the path and the dripping water behind him.

Two large boulders had fallen on the path ahead of him, forcing him to squeeze between them. Once through he found himself gazing into a large cavern.

Hesitating only a moment, he lowered himself to the cavern floor. Dim light was coming from somewhere, so he switched off his flashlight. He looked up and saw snow falling through a large opening above.

Steven heard loud squeals, and then wings flapping. He drew back at the sight of bats, hundreds of them, hanging from the ceiling and walls and flying in the dark above him. He did not want to disturb them.

Some bats were circling closer.

Steven knew he couldn't leave. He had to explore every nook and cranny in the cave to locate the dragon. The cave walls, the flapping wings of the bats, the horrible smells, were making him uneasy. He looked up and saw the eyes of the crows now staring down at him from the opening above like hungry vultures. It was all getting to him. This whole trip his fear has been building up to an explosion "That's it!" Steven cried out. "Boom! Boom! Boom!"

Instantly hundreds of bats took to the sky. Their loud screeches echoing off the cavern walls.

"What'd I do?" Steven asked, jumping to the ground, curling in a ball and covering his head, as hundreds of bats whipped against his body. He felt their wings fluttering against his shirt. *Do bats bite?* He covered his hair and waved his flashlight to protect himself.

The crows sprang from their perches, filling the air with their cawing as they flew into the opening of the cavern. The air was alive with bats and birds circling and diving, the noise incredible.

Steven remained on the ground as the crows pounced on the bats and chased them out of the cavern.

The chamber became quiet. It was dead quiet. Steven peered up cautiously. No bats. No crows.

Still shaken, Steven got to his knees. The crows had chased away the bats. Strange, he thought, and stood up, leaning against the wall.

He glanced at his watch. There was still time.

Steven headed toward the far wall of the cavern. He thought he heard a noise. He stopped moving

A snorting sound came from behind him.

Steven froze. Not hearing anything more, he cautiously continued walking, eyes searching in all directions. Where was that darn dragon?

A warm blast of air startled him. He listened again, yet all was very still. When he felt another gust of warm air against his back, he breathed a huge sigh of relief. "I'm glad you're here, Shu," Steven said, turning to greet his friend, the wind god. "You're not Shu," he gasped, jumping back, falling against the rock wall.

The dragon, stretching its long neck, moved its massive head to within inches of Steven's face.

Steven, eyes wide with fear, was staring into the dragon's eyes. Neither moved.

The dragon let out a low long growl, teeth bared.

Steven couldn't move. He was so close he could feel his hair moving every time the monstrous creature exhaled. "Seeker, where are you," he said, unable to believe the size of this ferocious-looking dragon.

The dragon reared back on its hind legs and let out a terrible roar. Smoke streamed from its nostrils and a fireball was building up inside its mouth.

Steven felt the heat and wanted to run, but there was no space in which to duck away from the beast now glaring at him with fire-red eyes.

"I'm not here to hurt you," Steven shouted, but his cry was drowned out by the roaring of the dragon.

Steven reached his hand to his backpack. If he could reach the flare gun...

The smoke was rising in thicker columns.

Steven's fingers played with the latch of the pack. A finger felt the barrel of his gun. A few more seconds and the gun would be in his hand. "Don't you know who I am?" He shouted, fingers unable to pull the gun from the pack still strapped to his back.

The amulet fell out of his shirt. It was glowing bright blue lighting up the whole cave.

The dragon pulled back slightly. "You are the boy?"

Steven could not understand her. All he knew was he was face-to-face with a massive creature whose power he couldn't even guess at, but who no longer appeared to want to attack him. He lowered his hand, hoping the dragon would see he wasn't a threat.

The dragon stepped closer dragging steel leg irons behind her.

Steven saw the irons and understood. Still frightened, knowing he could not escape if the creature attacked, he tried to sound confident, "Dragon, I am here to free you."

The dragon growled again, not understanding English.

Steven anxiously rubbed the amulet hanging over his shirt. It was a nervous habit, but suddenly he felt the blue stone grow warm.

The dragon stared at the stone which was now glowing with a sky-blue light. She stopped growling.

Steven was terrified but couldn't give up. "I said, I'm here to free you. I was sent by The Seeker."

"What did you say? You were sent by whom?"

"I understand you? You spoke English?" He saw the smoke was no longer rising from the dragon's nostrils. He let out a relieved sigh, but still watched closely for any sign of attack.

"Yes, I did," replied the dragon. "Do you speak dragon?"

Steven shook his head. "We don't have any dragons in the United States." He looked at the amulet and wondered if somehow it was responsible for allowing him to understand the dragon.

The dragon sighed. "Nor many elsewhere either. Now tell me, who is The Seeker?"

Steven stepped closer to the dragon. "He sent me here to release you, to set you free."

The dragon peered down at the boy. "How do I know you are telling the truth?"

Steven thought for a moment. "If you are not sure then you can kill me," Steven replied.

The dragon looked Steven up and down with his red eyes. "Yes, I could do that at any time."

Steven looked at his watch. "I don't have much time left. Can I please free you so I can go home?"

"Yes. Of course. Please release me," the dragon said, still uncertain of Steven's intentions.

Wisely afraid of the giant creature, Steven continued to speak to it as he examined the leather harness strapped around her head. "Who did this to you?" he asked, wondering how he was ever going to free this dragon.

The dragon didn't answer. She didn't like the boy coming this close to her. She had learned not to trust any humans.

"I'm not going to harm you," said Steven, as he moved his head around the dragon's long snout to get a better look. "By the way, do you have a name?" Slowly he raised his hand toward the massive head.

The dragon scraped her claw on the cavern floor.

Steven looked down. He saw a wide steel ankle bracelet attached to the dragon's leg. The skin around the steel bracelet was raw and blood was still oozing from open wounds. "You poor thing. Easy," he said in as soothing a voice as he could muster while facing a dragon. He crouched and placed his hand on the injured leg, then slid his palm down toward her ankle.

The dragon stood still, surprised at the tenderness the boy was showing toward her. "Morag," she said softly. "My name is Morag."

The boy looked up and smiled.

Morag wondered what the boy could do to remove the bonds that held her in captivity.

Steven wasn't sure either. The Amulet, now glowing blue, rested against his shirt. He didn't bother tucking it back but continued to move his hand toward the metal lock holding the strap around the dragon's ankle. "It's a thick lock and chain, Morag," he said.

The dragon nodded her head and snorted. "I have tried to open it. I'm afraid nothing will work."

Steven touched the lock with his fingers and was surprised to hear a loud click.

The lock snapped open.

"How in heck did that happen?" he said quickly removing the lock and pulling open the ankle bracelet, which dropped to the floor. Realizing a freed dragon could be seriously dangerous, he stepped back, raising his eyes to the monstrous mouth. Was she going to hurt him now that she was free?

Morag wore a bewildered expression as she backed away from the bracelet and looked down at her ankle. A tear fell from her eye as she sat back on her haunches.

Steven, relieved that she appeared not to want to hurt him said, "Bend your head down so I can remove the leather straps now."

The dragon cocked her head to one side not sure she understood his request.

"Bring your head down." Steven motioned with his hands.

Morag slowly lowered her head toward Steven.

Steven noticed the Amulet was again glowing bright blue as he reached for the lock on the harness. *Does the Amulet have anything to do with me being able to free the dragon?* Gently touching the lock, he heard a snap. The lock fell to the ground and he reached up and removed the leather harness from around the dragon's head.

"There," Steven said, dropping the straps to the floor.

The dragon backed up.

Steven felt nervous again.

The dragon lowered her head. "My name is Morag. What is your name, boy?"

"I am called Steven. How long have you been chained up in this cavern?"

"Three days I think. She looked at Steven and said, I was sent on a mission, to find a boy... such as you."

"By the Ruler of Darkness?" Steven felt his body tense. If the dragon had been sent after him, he would have to destroy her.

The dragon's head shot up. "Yes. Do you know of him?"

Steven moved away, backing toward the rock wall and exit. "Is the Dark Ruler here?" Steven looked anxiously around the cavern.

"He is not here, Steven. He sent his slave, The Slayer, and a bat called Batena. The slayer has gone hunting," Morag sniffed at Steven and then spoke again, "I sense that you are the boy we have been searching for? Is that correct?"

Steven felt fear race through his body. He wondered if he could run fast enough to escape this beast. He backed away, ready to break into a run.

"Wait! I will not harm you. The Ruler of Darkness has held me captive. You have freed me from his control. You have nothing to fear from me."

Steven turned back toward Morag. "Then we must leave while Drooling Slayer and Batena are gone. I've gotta find my friend Rusty and return to the village before he comes looking for me and sees you."

Just then, Steven heard Rusty calling his name.

"Coming!" Steven called back, hoping he could prevent Rusty from entering the cavern.

Too late!

"Where have you been?" Rusty demanded. "We were to meet thirty minutes ago at the entrance. Did you forget?"

Steven didn't move, waiting for Rusty to react to the sight of Morag towering over them in the cave.

"Let's go," Rusty commanded, turning around and heading out of the cavern. "Your aunt's going to kill us if we're late."

Steven was dumfounded. *How could he not see you?* Turning around, he was surprised to find Morag was gone and a large boulder was in her place. "Where did this come from?" he wondered.

As if in answer, a large eye opened in the middle of the boulder. "I am right here, Steven," Morag said, morphing back into her true shape.

"How did you do that?"

"Dragons can change their color to match their surroundings."

"You mean like a chameleon?"

"Yes"

"I guess there's a lot we don't know about dragons," Steven said.

"And much I do not know about humans," Morag replied, realizing this was the first human who had not tried to hurt or kill her.

"Steven, where the heck are you?" Rusty shouted.

"I'm right behind you, Rusty. I forgot my flashlight," Steven called. He turned back to Morag. "You have to get out of here now. Drooling Slayer mustn't find you when he returns. I'll contact The Seeker and we can come up with a plan to keep you safe. It is best that you remain out of sight until we decide what to do."

"I will do as you wish," Morag said.

"For now, move into the tunnel and hide until midnight tonight, then fly down to my hotel. It's the last one on the far side of town. I will be outside with a light and will flash it when I see you approach."

"I will be there at midnight. What's midnight?"

"Long after dark, and before the sun rises. You know, when the moon is in the center of the sky."

"Steven, where are you? We have to go!" Rusty shouted again.

Steven grabbed his backpack and charged back up the path to the entrance of the tunnel. "Let's go," he shouted, as he raced down the mountainside to retrieve his mountain bike.

"Now you're rushing?" Rusty asked, trying to keep up.

"Snow, rain, fog! We'd better get back to Glen Coe before the weather closes in again!" Steven threw his leg over the seat and pushed hard on the pedals.

All the way down the mountain, he checked the sky, not for the weather, but wondering if he would see Morag soaring above the clouds. Just what I need, he thought, a dragon. How am I going to ever hide a dragon from Aunt Celia?

Chapter 21

A cold rain started just as Steven and Rusty biked back to the Inn. They were soaked by the time they arrived.

Steven was drying his hair when he heard a knock at the door.

"Steven," Aunt Celia called.

"Just a minute." Steven walked over to open the door.

His aunt stood smiling surrounded with packages on the floor and more bags hanging on her arms. "Help," Aunt Celia sputtered as a bag fell to the floor.

Steven laughed as he picked up the package. "You're wet! Looks like you're about ready to drop from shopping too!"

Aunt Celia sighed. "I guess I did get a bit carried away." She shook her head. "I'm going to put these in my room and get cleaned up before we head out for dinner. I booked our reservation at the Carnoch Restaurant for 5:30. I will meet you two downstairs in thirty minutes."

"We'll be ready to go." Steven watched her maneuver down the hallway with all the boxes. "Need help?"

"No, I've got it," she said as another box fell to the floor.

Laughing at her juggling, Steven closed the door.

Rusty came out of the bathroom vigorously rubbing a white towel over his hair. "Great shower! Who was that?"

"Aunt Celia. She'll meet us in twenty-five minutes for dinner, so get jumping into some clothes."

Arriving at the restaurant on time, they headed into the dining room. The wood panels were decorated with faded paintings. Steven was surprised to see some that looked like knights fighting with dragons, the dragons never winning against swords and arrows. He sat through the entire meal worried about Morag. It was difficult to concentrate on anything Rusty and Aunt Celia were talking about. He was hoping the dragon wouldn't show up. That would really mess things up.

"Steven? Steven?" Aunt Celia was poking him gently. "Where are you this evening?"

"He's been like this since we left the cave today," Rusty said.

"Cave? You two went onto a cave? Don't you think that was dangerous without adult supervision?

"It was a large cave and quite easy to walk through," Steven said, still thinking what would have happen if the Slayer found him with Morag. "Maybe we should return the bikes tomorrow morning. I heard the weatherman forecast high winds and rain squalls tomorrow," he said, hoping Rusty would agree. He did not want his friend exposed to more danger.

"Not a good day to ride the trails for sure," Rusty said.

"I have an idea. Why not get up early tomorrow morning and drive back to Edinburgh? We could be there around noon which would give us an opportunity to explore more of the city." Steven watched for his aunt's reaction.

"I thought you wanted to explore the mountains?" Aunt Celia said.

Steven nodded. "I saw a lot today and it was a bit steep."

"That was one tough ride," Rusty agreed. "I'm with Steven on this one."

Yes! Steven thought. The faster we get away from here the less chance of getting caught in this mess. "Edinburgh has great stores…"

Aunt Celia smiled. "Great idea! We'll leave early and find a hotel for tomorrow night. I can't wait to find a Mill Shop."

"Here we go again, Steven," Rusty groaned. "More shopping!"

As the evening grew darker, the weather worsened. Steven felt a little safer knowing that any markings they had left behind on the trail would be washed away by the rain. He wondered if Morag was safe.

She's a dragon, he told himself, but then remembered she had been imprisoned by the Dark Ruler and tormented by some creature called Drooling Slayer. He kept looking at his watch, hoping Morag would show up at the appointed time.

When they arrived back at the inn, they went into the lounge to listen to a bag piper. At first, Steven wasn't crazy about the sound, but soon felt better about the noisy instrument. He hoped the piper's loud music would hide the sound of dragon wings should Morag appear before midnight.

****

Steven woke up before his alarm went off, which was good. He saw Rusty was still sound asleep, arms wrapped around his pillow. The clock on the lamp table read, 11:45. Howling winds still beat against the window, but the rain had stopped. Could a dragon fly in wind and rain?

Steven rolled out of bed and got dressed. He grabbed his phone and flashlight, and, opening the door to the hall, paused to listen. All in the inn appeared to be asleep. He wished he was.

Steven walked through the lobby and out the back door. Moving away from the building, he headed toward the fenced-in field. The scent of rain still lingered.

Standing next to a fencepost, he waited impatiently for Morag to arrive, looking frequently around the hotel back yard and fields surrounding the Inn. He wanted to make sure it was safe to open the Portal. All appeared quiet; no lights were visible from any of the windows of the hotel. Scanning the sky, he waited anxiously for Morag's arrival, wondering if the dragon had decided to not risk getting help from a human and had escaped on her own.

Steven's ears picked up a whooshing sound. He turned in the direction of the noise and saw a black dot in the distance. It was her. Morag was soaring over the hill. He flashed his light into the sky.

Morag headed toward him.

Her wingspan must be at least 50 feet across. Steven felt frightened as the huge beast approached. What if she wasn't as friendly as he hoped?

Morag landed gently on the ground near him.

"I'm glad you're here," Steven said, hoping she was still friendly.

Morag nodded her head. "It is good to see you too, boy."

Steven hadn't realized just how large Morag was. Now he did. "How am I going to get you home? You're too big," Steven said, realizing he hadn't thought this out fully.

"I can help."

Steven turned and saw The Seeker materializing next to him. "Thank goodness you're here. You have no idea what I've been through."

"There will be time to talk later, but for now—" The Seeker raised his arms toward Morag. "Bashum."

Morag shivered and within a few seconds shrank down to the size of a large cat. She looked stunned, shooting her head in all directions.

"She's small?" Steven exclaimed, now towering over the dragon. "How did you do that?" he asked, not believing he was looking down at Morag. "That's a lot better. How long will she remain this size?"

"She can transform herself when she likes," The Seeker replied.

"A dragon who can shrink to the size of a large cat. Cool!" Now, I've seen everything."

The Seeker smiled. "Not quite everything."

Steven frowned. "You're right. Now, where were you when I needed you?"

"I knew you could handle a mere dragon and I had important errands to run. In fact, I must leave again," The Seeker said, "I will join you back at the lab in a few days."

"Wait a minute!"

It was too late. The Seeker disappeared.

"I wish I could do that," Steven said, gazing down at Morag who seemed quite content with her new size.

Steven took the phone from his pocket and pressed the Portal App.

He signaled Morag. "You have to follow me. I'll explain everything after we're safe."

The portal appeared, much to Steven's relief.

Morag jumped back at the strange object.

Steven stepped into the shimmering pool of light. "It's safe. It won't hurt you," he urged.

Morag craned her neck at the portal, and then, apparently feeling she could trust this boy, followed him into the sphere of swirling light.

Within seconds, Steven and Morag were back in the lab.

Morag snorted at the Portal.

Steven walked over to the wall and turned on the lights. He then rushed to the computer and closed the Portal.

Morag was startled by its disappearance but was more curious about her new surroundings. She had never been in a human home before. "Is this a cave?" She asked.

Steven laughed. "No. It's my house. And this is my parents' lab."

Morag wandered toward the table.

"And don't touch anything," Steven warned, realizing a dragon could cause all kinds of havoc in a laboratory.

Morag jumped back into the center of the room, looking upset.

Steven sighed. "I'm sorry. I'll show you everything later, but first, there are some things I have to know." He gave her a kind look. "Did you see Drooling Slayer after I left the cave?"

Morag sat on her haunches. "No. I neither saw the monster, nor picked up his scent. As soon as you left me, I flew down from the mountain and followed along the water. I stopped only to drink and feed."

"Feed?" Steven had not thought about what he could feed a dragon. "Morag, for the time being, you'll be safe here. Drooling Slayer and the Ruler of Darkness don't know who I am nor about this place."

Morag's ears rose. "Steven, we're not alone. I smell another life here."

Steven tensed. Could he have been wrong? Could he have been found out already? "I need to check out the rest of the house. I will give you a quick run through the house because I must get back to Glen Coe before Rusty and my aunt wake up," Steven said, as he opened the lab door.

Morag followed a few steps behind.

Steven walked down the hall, and up the stairs into the kitchen. "Tuck up your wings and watch your tail. I don't want you to knock over furniture or lamps."

"Furniture, lamps?"

"I will show you before I go."

"I must remain alone here?"

"Yes. But only until I return. No one except The Seeker, Bastet, and now, you, know that I have the ability to transport across space using the Portal. If my aunt found out, it could put her in danger."

Morag stopped walking. "Steven, I have picked up that scent again."

Just then, Bastet came charging into the kitchen and jumped up on the counter followed by a shrill scream.

Morag exposed her teeth.

Bastet, back arched, hair standing up along her back, glared at Morag, growling menacingly.

"Bastet!" Steven shouted. "Quiet! Leave her alone!"

Bastet showed her claws, nails razor-sharp.

Morag moved closer, her teeth preparing to bite down hard on this threat to Steven.

"Both of you stop now!"

Bastet was still glaring but pulled back her claws.

Morag refused to move away.

Steven sighed. "Morag, this is Bastet, my cat."

Bastet grumbled, *I'm much more than a mere cat, boy.*

Steven didn't hear her. "And Bastet, this is Morag a new member of our home and a friend."

Bastet looked up at Steven then back to Morag. Slowly her back flattened and she sat on the counter.

"Pleased to meet you, Bastet."

I can understand you, meowed Bastet.

"Bastet, Aunt Celia hasn't returned from our trip to Scotland yet. She has no idea I'm here. I needed to get Morag away from the Drooling Slayer," Steven said.

At the name Morag shivered.

Steven said, "Please take care of Morag while I'm gone?"

Now I'm a baby-sitter for a dragon? Bastet fumed.

"Where am I going to stay?" asked Morag.

"I can't allow you to move around the house. For now, let's take you back down to the lab."

A low rumble came from Morag's stomach. She looked embarrassed, "I'm a bit hungry," she muttered.

Don't look at me, Bastet said, backing away. *A hungry dragon? That's just what I need.*

"Can you wait until I return? We'll figure out something then."

"Yes, I will try, but upon your return I must hunt. I only eat living creatures."

Steven sighed. This hero stuff was getting more and more complicated. What next?

Chapter 22

Steven felt uneasy about leaving Morag with Bastet in the lab but couldn't think of anything else he could do with a dragon. He called back the Portal and it zipped him back to Scotland. He could hardly keep his eyes open as he made it disappear and snuck back into the inn.

He just made it into his bed when Rusty woke with a loud yawn and ran into the bathroom.

No sleep tonight, I guess, Steven thought. Hearing the water running, Steven sat up in bed thinking about the problems a dragon could cause if he didn't get back as soon as possible.

Rusty, finished with the bathroom, sat down on his bed. "What a dream I had! I was fast asleep when I found myself standing at the window. I was staring at this strange object…a white rotating globe."

Steven froze. Had Rusty seen the Portal?

Rusty shrugged. "At least I think it was a globe. It just seemed to hover over the grass…like on 'Stargate'. You know?"

"Maybe you were watching an old movie or something," Steven said, giving an uneasy laugh.

Rusty shook his head. "You were in the dream. You were looking at your smart phone. I called to you, but you didn't answer. Suddenly you stepped into this globe-thing and 'poof'! You were gone."

"Now, I know you're crazy," Steven laughed again.

Rusty eyed Steven. "The next thing I remember is sitting up in bed and when I looked over at you, you were asleep."

"Like I said, you've been watching too much of that TV program,"

Steven said, laughing, but worried Rusty might share his dream with his aunt.

Rusty was still staring at Steven. "I know I was dreaming, but it was so real…"

Steven got out of bed and entered the bathroom while Rusty continued to jabber about teleporting. *Boy, was that close! Imagine if he'd seen the dragon!*

****

"Are you sure you are feeling all right, Steven?" Aunt Celia asked as they drove out of Edinburg after breakfast.

"I'm fine," Steven replied.

Aunt Celia didn't look convinced. She thought Steven looked as if he hadn't slept. "Well boys, all good things must come to an end. Tomorrow, we fly home. Did you have a good vacation?"

"It was fantastic," Rusty said, and chattered away about all the fun things he did in Scotland.

Steven sank back into the seat and thought about all he had experienced. "It really was something," he said when his aunt looked at him in the mirror.

The drive in the rain was uneventful, though the closer they got to the city, the more anxious Steven got. What if the dragon wrecked his lab? What if Bastet and Morag didn't get along? And worse yet, she couldn't wait another day to eat. He wished he could share his fears with his aunt, or even Rusty, but had to comfort himself by repeating that soon they would return home. That couldn't come soon enough for him.

****

After having dinner in Boston, Steven and his aunt arrived home at 9:00 pm. Steven waited impatiently for Aunt Celia to fumble with her keys and open the door. He was relieved when he heard Bastet meowing, but wondered if Morag was still in the hiding in the lab.

Dragging the luggage into the foyer, Steven looked around the first floor, hoping Morag was not going to charge out to greet them. He let out a huge sigh of relief when Bastet came rushing over, meowed and started to sniff the luggage.

"I guess your cat is glad to see you," Aunt Celia said.

"Aunt Celia, I'll take my stuff up and come back to help you with yours, okay?"

"Thanks, Steven, but I can take care of them. I want to remove some of the items I bought before taking the bags upstairs. Go ahead up. And try to relax. It's been a long day and you look tired."

Not needing to be told twice, Steven took his luggage to his room and closed the door behind him.

Bastet jumped onto the bed. *Boy am I glad you're home,* she meowed. *That dragon would not stay in the lab.*

"Morag?" Steven whispered, glancing around the room.

Come out, you clumsy dragon, Bastet mewed.

Morag walked out of the bathroom and sat next to the bed.

Steven shook his head. "You were to stay in the lab. Did anyone see you?"

Yes, Bastet meowed.

"No … well maybe," Morag said, looking sheepishly at the floor.

"Well is it yes or no?" Steven asked.

"Not sure," Morag replied.

Steven sighed. "Bastet, what happened?"

Bastet shook her head. *You forgot to warn us that nosy Mrs. Parker had the key to the house.*

"Oh no." Steven groaned.

We were upstairs sleeping. I was on the windowsill and your dragon friend was on the floor. I jumped up when I heard someone climbing the stairs. As I hurried to get this clumsy beast into the bathroom, I heard Mrs. Parker make a gasping noise and run out of the room.

Steven gazed at Morag. "If she saw you, she'll tell my aunt."

Sorry, Steven, Bastet said, thinking dragons are trouble.

"Nothing we can do about this but wait." Steven sat down on the floor between them, falling back against the bed. "Good to be home, though." He glanced at the dragon. "Morag, until I hear from The Seeker what to do with you, I think you need to stay here."

Morag nodded her head. "I too think that would be best for now. Bastet tells me your next quest is to Mount Li. That is where I was taken from my mother by that creature you call Drooling Slayer. I want to go back and search for her. I can help you with your mission."

Steven studied the small dragon. "Okay, I guess that's why The Seeker sent me to free you. I can certainly use another friend now that I am involved in the prophecy."

"I'll be most helpful," Morag promised. "But I must return to China to search for my mother."

Morag's stomach rumbled loudly. "I need to feed soon."

You always need to feed, Bastet grumbled.

"I'm a growing dragon."

Don't grow around here. You'll destroy the house, Bastet growled.

"Enough! We must work together. Morag tonight, you are free to feed, but you must only fly at night, preferably when there isn't a full moon. People mustn't see you, especially my aunt. Only change to your normal size in unpopulated areas."

"I understand and will be extremely careful not to be seen or heard. I only need to feed twice a week. Bastet says there are ample rodents, turkeys, and waterfowl in this area."

I said that, so she wouldn't eat me, Bastet grumbled again.

"I don't dine on my friends," Morag said softly.

Bastet just meowed.

Steven nodded. "There is enough deer to the north that should satisfy your hunger. How will you find your food?"

Morag smiled. "I sense heat sources. This will also help me to avoid humans. You give off a lot of heat."

"But deer only. You must promise not to hunt livestock."

"Livestock? I've never heard of such an animal."

Steven laughed. "Farm animals: Chickens, ducks, cows, horses, etc. If farmers start losing their livestock, they'll call the police and start hunting for whatever is killing their animals."

"That would be bad," Morag said.

Steven nodded. "And, if Drooling Slayer, or the Dark Ruler hear farmers complaining that their livestock is disappearing, they may investigate and find out where I live."

"I will not let that happen," Morag promised.

"Good!"

"I will hunt in the forests, far away? Surely that will be safe?"

Steven thought about that. "The farther north you forage for food the less likely you will be seen. We can't take any chances. After you finish eating, you must drop the remainders in the ocean, or a deep pond. No one should be able to find the evidence of your existence."

Morag nodded.

"Alright. I know you are hungry, so just remember the rules and go have fun. You've been cooped up too long and while you are small you might become prey rather than the attacker." Steven said.

"Let them try." Morag stood and stretched her wings. "I will return long before dawn. I promise all will be well."

"Okay! There's no moon tonight. It's a good night to try this out, but remember, you must remain out of sight at all times and Aunt Celia must never, ever, never, see you so we'll wait until she's asleep."

It was after 10:00 when Aunt Celia went to bed and Steven opened the window.

"I will be very careful, Steven," Morag said as she prepared to leap from the window ledge.

Remember what the boy said, meowed Bastet.

Morag looked at Bastet and then at Steven. "I would never risk hurting him," she said, and spreading her wings launched herself into the air.

Steven watched as she gained altitude and disappeared into the night. Good Luck! Steven thought as he caught one last glimpse of her in flight.

I wonder how people would react to seeing a dragon suddenly appear in the night? Steven thought as he closed the screen. "On second thought, I hope I never have to find out."

Chapter 23

Drooling Slayer returned to the cave two days after Steven and his aunt left for Rhode Island. Stepping cautiously down the path toward the cavern floor, he stopped and looked for the dragon. Across his shoulders was the carcass of another deer. "Dragon," he bellowed, "I have brought fresh meat." He knew she sometimes camouflaged herself and began searching the area. "If you do not show yourself, I will not allow you to feed," he threatened, throwing the deer to the stone floor. He angrily slammed his club against the cave floor. "Get over here!" he yelled. "When I find you, I will beat you hard on your head!"

Drooling Slayer banged his club again. The steel ankle bracelet bounced into the air.

The Slayer rushed over and saw the leather harness was near the wall. He drew his knife and moved cautiously toward the wall, looking in every direction for the dragon, knowing the beast hated him because of the abuse he had inflicted on her over three years.

He kicked the chain. "How did she get loose?" he roared, moving slowly and checking the cavern floor for footprints. On closer inspection he found small footprints. They were small...too small for a dragon.

"Who did this?" he shouted, his face turning red with rage. "Can it be that the boy I am searching for has done this?" The Slayer sniffed the air but detected no human scent.

Drooling Slayer heard wings flapping over his head and looked up to be sure it wasn't an attacker. "I lost the dragon," he shouted, "Go and find her!"

"You lost the dragon?" Batena circled the Slayer.

"She must have been freed by that boy while I was out feeding last night." He pounded his club on the ground. "Wait until I get them."

"The Ruler will not be happy to hear this," Batena chirped, eager to see what punishment the brutal creature would receive once she ratted on him.

Drooling Slayer glared at the gleeful bat who did not even try to hide her smile. "I am sure you can't wait to inform him!" He snarled. "But wait! This proves the boy does not live in Egypt as the Ruler thought, but in Scotland. That is information he'll welcome." He breathed a sigh of relief. "Worthless bat, I want you to search the villages and the surrounding area for the boy and that dragon. How difficult can it be to find a monstrous dragon? While you conduct the search here, I will search the mountains. I know that dragon and she must be hungry by now. I'll find where she has fed. It can't be that far." Drooling Slayer kicked the thick chain again. "You will not tell anything to the Ruler until I say so."

The bat looked disappointed. "You mean you're not eager to see the Ruler with me?"

"If I don't find that dragon here, I will return to where I first encountered the beast. She may go there to search for her mother." He swung the club at the bat. "Now get out of here before I show you how I treat tattle-tales."

The bat squealed loudly and flew from the cave.

The Slayer stormed over to the deer carcass and dragged it to the fire pit in the corner. "There's no point in letting you go to waste," he said, picking kindling piled up on the floor. Just wait until I get my hands on that boy and dragon. His eyes were the same color as the fire.

Chapter 24

What a wonderful feeling to be free to fly without that harness and chain around me. Morag soared high above the trees. She had dreamed of this day for three years. She was grateful to the boy for releasing her. She knew the Slayer would have killed her eventually, either by starvation or by striking her with his club in a fit of temper. The young boy was unlike the humans her mother had warned of. She felt safe again. She was beginning to believe she would not have to worry about her safety as long as she remained with him.

As she was flying, her mind was returning to dark thoughts spawned by her past. *Our paths will cross again, Drooling Slayer! And when that day arrives, I will punish you for all you have inflicted upon me.*

Several thousand feet above the earth, Morag glided on updrafts as she searched the forest and fields. She flew over a large lake. After checking that no humans were near, she swooped down, diving into the depths of the cold water.

Rising to the surface, Morag splashed her wings, removing the filth accumulated on her body during her time of imprisonment. She reveled in the joy her new-found freedom brought.

Her splashing created enough noise to get the attention of nearby creatures. Miles away, dogs, hearing the unusual sounds, began barking. Lights went on in houses. Hunters grabbed their guns.

Morag was still frolicking in the water when she noticed lights appear along the far shoreline. She lowered herself in the murky lake and remained still. She realized she should have been more careful, especially in her full-size.

It seemed like hours until the lights moved away.

After letting more time pass, Morag cautiously moved toward shore. She checked in all directions, and then, convinced she was not being observed, took to the sky.

It was 5:00 in the morning when Morag returned to Steven's window. Bastet heard Morag approach and jumped up on the windowsill. Seeing the dragon was back, she pounced on the bed, then climbed up on Steven's chest. "Meow," she called, as she touched his nose with her paw. *The pest is back,* she yowled.

Steven snapped up into a sitting position. "Thanks, Bastet." He rolled out of bed and lifted the screen. Morag jumped into the room and flew to the bed.

Was your hunt successful? Bastet asked, realizing she missed hunting, but had sworn to protect the boy.

"Yes, it was wonderful. I was able to bathe and relish my new-found freedom. I had come to believe that I would never be free again." She sighed. "I have not known such joy since I was born."

Steven understood, sometimes feeling he couldn't be free, not with the prophecy governing his life. "When were you born?" he asked.

"My mother told me she dropped her egg almost ten years before I was hatched, somewhere beneath the tomb of Emperor Qin Shi Huang in Mount Li."

"Ten years?" Steven asked, a surprised expression on his face.

"Yes," answered Morag. "Mother protected it until the conditions were correct."

Steven scratched his head. "What conditions? You guys look so tough, like nothing can hurt you."

Morag smiled. "Dragons can only be born during thunder and lightning storms. The intensity of the storm must be strong enough to cause the egg to break open. The power of a dragon is measured by the severity of the storm required to crack its egg."

Bastet meowed, *Well, your storm must have been weak.*

Morag shook her head. "My mother waited over ten years for the right storm. She said as she placed my egg on the stone lintel above the tomb of the Emperor, the storm grew more and more powerful, with lightning crashing everywhere. She said the lintel glowed bright red and the wind howled like a wolf, rain pounding the earth."

Bastet thought what a show-off.

Morag continued, "Steam rose as lightning hit the ground. A huge, dark, cloud settled directly over my egg. The stone lintel repeatedly struck by lightning became boiling hot. Cracks appeared on my shell. Suddenly a large bolt of lightning raced down from the center of that huge cloud and struck the lintel with such force that the egg shattered, tossing me into the air."

"I never knew dragons had to go through so much to be born," Steven said.

Oh brother, Bastet thought, bored by the whole thing.

"Oh yes. It's quite amazing. After the egg was shattered and I was thrown into the air, my mother caught me before I was struck by lightning and killed. Holding me tightly, she reentered the Emperor's tomb." Morag looked sad. "She placed me on a bed of straw and waited and watched over me. She said that I did not move for three days and nights. She was quite worried, but on the morning of the fourth day, I stood up and looked directly at her with my blue sparkling eyes." She turned her eyes toward Steven.

"What a story," Steven said, thinking how he missed his mother and father.

What a story is right, Bastet thought, jealous the dragon was getting all the attention.

Just then there was a knock at the door.

"Quick! Hide, Morag!"

Morag scurried under the bed as the door opened.

"Good morning, Aunt Celia," Steven said, trying to look relaxed

"Was that Bastet who ran under the bed?" Aunt Celia asked, searching the floor.

"Yep. That was her." Steven laughed. "You know how she gets

sometimes ... chasing her tail, then charging around the place as if she were running for her life."

Bastet, who was listening, darted out from under the bed and raced across the floor, out into the hallway.

"See what I mean?" Steven said, shaking his head.

"Crazy cat. Well, come down for breakfast. It's all ready."

"I'll be there in a little while. I need to take a shower and unpack."

"See you soon," Aunt Celia said.

Just as she started to close the door, Bastet darted into the room and jumped up onto the comforter.

Aunt Celia looked confused, then laughed. "I wish I had her speed! Crazy cat! Don't be long, dear." She shook her head and closed the door.

"The coast is clear," Steven said.

"That was close," Morag said as she jumped up on the bed.

Steven wondered how much longer he could keep Aunt Celia in the dark, especially with a dragon in the house.

Chapter 25

Steven and Bastet hurried back to the lab after breakfast. Morag was carefully tucked in Steven's backpack.

While the three were talking, Morag suddenly unfurled her wings and stood on her hind legs. She looked across the room and growled a warning.

Steven turned to see what she was looking at, and The Seeker materialized.

"Good morning," said The Seeker.

Morag folded her wings and lay down on the table.

"What a beautiful dragon you are Morag," The Seeker said as he moved over to examine her. "I can tell that you will develop into a strong dragon. Your talons are well formed. The sharp spines on your back and your long tail will provide excellent protection in battle. How old are you?"

"I am in my third year and within two years of being fully grown."

The Seeker looked into her eyes. "I think the best solution now is for you to remain the size of a cat here and while flying to and from Steven's home."

Morag looked surprised.

"Would you agree to that?" The Seeker asked. "You could stay with Steven then."

Morag stared at The Seeker and then turned to Steven. She let out a deep sigh. "I don't know. I like being large. Dragons are meant to be enormous. And eating rodents does not satisfy me." She snorted. "It's a bit below my dignity, you know."

Steven nodded his head. "If you remained at this size you would be able to move around the house and search for food undetected by other humans. You'd look like a large bird of prey." Steven laughed. "I don't know about traveling in the car though."

"Car?"

"I'll show you later. Aunt Celia and I are planning a day trip in a few weeks. Bastet and you will join us if you can stay small." He stroked Morag's neck. "Yup, keeping you the size of a cat would solve a lot of problems."

Morag sighed again. "Can I still change to my normal size?"

The Seeker nodded. "Yes. But only when you are well away from this house."

"Then I shall say, 'okay'," as Steven says. Morag smiled.

"Then you shall become part of our team," The Seeker said.

"Yes, if you will allow me," Morag responded.

"Then it is agreed," The Seeker said. "You will be the fourth member of the team. Now that all this is settled, I am curious. Your long neck and pointed snout show you to be a western dragon. How did you come to be living in Asia?"

"My mother told me that the Asian people did not fear us as did those in the west. Europeans have hunted us to near extinction. She wanted to raise me free of the constant fear of being hunted and killed."

The Seeker nodded. "The four of us will be a formidable team as we continue our search for the Guardians."

Steven nodded in agreement.

The Seeker's face grew serious. "Now to matters of grave concern. From what I have heard, Drooling Slayer—"

Morag stood back on her hind legs and bellowed loudly.

Steven jumped. "No Morag. Shhh."

The Seeker eyed the dragon. "I understand your disgust. I promise his deeds will not go unpunished."

Morag sat back on her haunches.

The Seeker continued, "Drooling Slayer has remained in the highlands still searching for you. We need not concern ourselves with him or Campbell now that we have Morag free. What does concern me now is that another servant of the Ruler of Darkness has been pressed into service to search for Steven."

"Not another one?" Steven now looked disgusted.

The Seeker frowned. "Steven, she is a small bat known as Batena."

"A bat? No biggie," Steven said.

The Seeker wasn't sure what that meant. "The Ruler is using this bat to communicate with Drooling Slayer. She is one of his best spies."

"But she's only a bat," Steven said.

The Seeker looked at Morag and said, "Never underestimate an enemy because of their size. Batena knows what you look like."

"How did she find out?" Steven erupted. "I don't remember seeing a bat in any of my adventures."

"She was sleeping in Seti's chamber when we entered the tomb. I sensed her presence as she spied on us from a high corner of the room."

"Why didn't you say something? We could have stopped her." Steven clenched his fists.

"She flew into a vent as we released the Guardian. At the time, I didn't think it was that important; but I've seen her several times while you were in the highlands. The only explanation is she must be helping the Ruler search for you."

Morag growled angrily. "The Seeker is correct, Steven. The bat did accompany Drooling Slayer from the Ruler's Mountain to Egypt and then to Scotland. I never understood why until now."

"This bat must be stopped before she finds out where I live," Steven said. "It can't be that hard to catch a bat. Is it?"

Morag spoke up. "I can set a trap for her when we arrive at the tomb."

The Seeker nodded, "I forgot to tell you one detail. She's a vampire bat. She needs blood to survive."

Steven shivered. "That's disgusting."

Morag was thinking. "Very well, for Steven, I will make the sacrifice. I will cut my lip. When she smells the fresh blood dripping from the cut she will seek me out. Once she lands close enough, I will snap my jaws around her and no more bat."

Steven shook his head. "Won't she know it's you?"

"She will not know until my jaws lock around her. The bat has never seen me as I am now."

Steven was grateful the dragon wanted to help but wondered if a dragon the size of a cat could really take on a blood-sucking bat servant of The Dark Ruler. He had already grown fond of Morag and didn't want to lose her.

The storm clouds were shooting lightning bolts down on Rhode Island with incredible fury. Even safe in his room, Steven shuddered at their violence.

Morag lay on the foot of his bed while Bastet was sitting alert at the window, eyes peering into the storm, ready to lay down her life to protect Steven from any demonic being that could be hiding in the storm.

Steven saw shadows on the wall. They appeared to be moving like ghosts lit up by the flashes of lightning. He knew they weren't real, but why did they remind him of the Guardians with their skeletal bodies and blazing red eyes? He promised he would not be afraid of the lightning and thunder but wondered if he had the courage to truly be the boy of the prophecy. He knew the next mission was coming soon and he had to be ready to face whatever demons the Dark Ruler sent to defeat him.

The End

Can Steven fight his fear and defeat the Dark Ruler? What is Morag's secret that will force her to risk her life? The next exciting adventure for Steven will take him to the Carlsbad Caverns in New Mexico 1,604 feet below the surface of the earth. The Guardian deep below the earth is his next challenge. Will Steven overcome the Ruler's slaves and servants?

Find out in Steven's next adventure: The Guardian of Carlsbad Caverns.

More from AimHi Press and Newhouse Creative Group

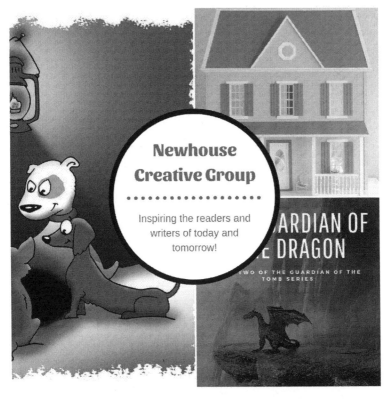

Visit AimHiPress.com for more books and other products from AimHi Press, NCG Key, and the rest of the Newhouse Creative Group family!

About the Author

William S. Russell and his wife live in The Villages, Florida. He is a member of the Writers 4 Kids and the Writers League of the Villages. Although he has never traveled to Egypt, the Egyptian architecture, inscriptions, language and culture have always intrigued him.

Made in the USA
Columbia, SC
23 February 2019